THE HEAT OF ANGELS

Praise for Lisa Girolami

Love on Location is "an explosive and romantic story set in the world of movies."—*Divadirect.co.uk*

"The women of *Run to Me* are multi-dimensional and the running metaphor is well placed throughout this tale. Girolami has given us an entertaining story that makes us think—about relationships, about running away, and about what we want to run to in our lives."—*Just About Write*

Jane Doe "is one of those quiet books that ends up getting under your skin. The story flowed with the ease of a slow-moving river. All in all a well-written story with an unusual setting, and well worth the read."—*Lambda Literary Foundation*

"*Jane Doe* is a lovely, easy to read romance that left me with a smile on my face."—*Just About Write*

In *The Pleasure Set* "Girolami has done a wonderful job portraying the wealthy dilettantes along with the complex characters of Laney and Sandrine. Her villain is a great combination of brains and ruthlessness. Of course, the sex scenes are fabulous. This novel is a great blend of sex, romance, and mystery, and the cover…is perfect."—*Just About Write*

By the Author

Love on Location

Run to Me

The Pleasure Set

Jane Doe

Fugitives of Love

Cut to the Chase

The Heat of Angels

Visit us at www.boldstrokesbooks.com

THE HEAT OF ANGELS

by

Lisa Girolami

2014

THE HEAT OF ANGELS

ISBN 13: 978-1-62639-042-3

This Trade Paperback Original Is Published By
Bold Strokes Books, Inc.
P.O. Box 249
Valley Falls, NY 12185

First Edition: March 2014

CREDITS
Editor: Shelley Thrasher
Production Design: Stacia Seaman
Cover Design by Sheri (graphicartist2020@hotmail.com)

Acknowledgments

My deepest gratitude to Shelley for her never-wavering support.

Many thanks to Kari for advising me on the K9 sections and keeping them real.

And a big huzzah to my readers, who are the absolute best.

For Abel, K9 officer and partner (2004–2009):

For your service to, and protection of,
Deputy Sheriff Kari Cranfill and all of Riverside County.
You will never be forgotten.

PROLOGUE

I'm not safe.

Noises came from somewhere close by, but they were muffled. Four of her senses had seemed to die away, leaving only the one most suitable for her survival. She registered sounds as a deer would scrutinize the approaching footsteps of a predator.

The smack of something against wood. Two people talking. Maybe three. Someone slamming a cabinet door.

The strain of listening added to the fear that already robbed her airways, allowing only short staccato breaths to keep her conscious.

Was that someone opening a door? It was hard to say because a television was turned up pretty loud. It had to be after seven in the evening because of the shows she could hear. First, the laughs from some comedy show shook the air, but she couldn't tell which one it was. After that, she could make out the game show *Family Feud*, followed by *Wheel of Fortune*. Then the news came on and had been on for a while.

She didn't have enough light to ascertain her environment beyond unfamiliar furniture and windows facing maybe a forest. Her nose picked something up. What? Smells of fresh cigarettes mingled with the stench of old trash.

She'd been sitting there for hours and had no idea what to do.

"Please come get me."

Her eyes were puffy from crying, and a headache knifed the back of her right eye. She stretched, but her muscles felt like they were on fire.

I don't understand, she thought. What happened?

She rubbed her eye, trying to push the pain farther back so it wasn't right at the front of her skull.

The television went silent.

She leaned forward, listening and trying to picture the room outside her door.

She was in a lot of trouble. She'd give anything for it to be about five hours ago, when she was back at school with her friends, hanging out in the hall and contemplating a smoke in the girls' room.

Subdued conversation came from just outside her door.

Now I'm really fucked, she thought.

I'm not safe.

CHAPTER ONE

The skies over Los Angeles had persisted to be a haze of angry amber for days. Like a brown bear, livid from an interrupted slumber, fire season had awoken swiftly. The first week of June had just passed, and every sign indicated that the residents of the City of Angels would see more blackened hills than usual. Significant fires were already raging in four "urban interface areas," the coveted heights above the city where the homes of the affluent sat upon brush-covered canyons and hillsides. Never mind that these natural areas had historically burned long before homes were built; the views were just too tempting.

Chris Bergstrom shifted in the seat of her squad car in an attempt to dry the dampness of her sweaty thighs. The thermometer on her dash registered ninety-one degrees, and though it was exactly one o'clock in the afternoon, the smoke-filled air shrouded the city streets in a murky veil of uneasy apprehension.

Her job as a K9 police officer wasn't to fight the fires, but keep the streets of L.A. as calm as possible. But the outbreaks kicking up in the hills around the city made everyone nervous. Sure, people went about their day, but the constant reminder that the hot, dry Santa Ana winds were showing no signs of simmering down kept everyone's eyes on the smoke. And just as the citizens she protected worked that Friday afternoon, so did the criminals.

A whine came from her backseat. Abel, her K9 partner,

was more agitated than usual. The seventy-five-pound Belgian Malinois snorted and then barked.

Chris told him to stop and he replied with another whine.

"I know the smoke is bad, buddy," she said as she punched a few buttons on her dash computer. "We've got three more hours, so settle down, okay?"

But Chris knew those three hours would turn out like the last seven. Fires brought out all the crazies. These shifts were no different than the ones that fell on the full moon, any professional-championship game night, and all holidays except, for some reason, Kwanzaa. Flames attracted people just as flash floods did. Rapidly rising waters and swiftly approaching brush fires seemed to lure knuckleheads, piper-like, to flirt with their luck. And those particular nights were always busy with idiots who didn't know when to stay away.

Her screen blipped and she scanned the text. Turning north on the next street, she pulled her bulletproof vest away from her shirt to encourage the heat to escape.

"We're heading up to Runyon Canyon, Abel. An upstanding citizen is waiting for our assistance."

❖

Sarah Pullman finished washing down the concrete pathway in front of the cougar enclosures. They watched her with little more attention than they would an aimless metallic fig beetle buzzing around their habitat.

She curled the hose back up at one of the many faucets smartly laid out about a hundred feet from each other and made her way to the next one to wash down the pathway near Samuel, the lion. When she turned the hose on, he sleepily raised his head and she called out to him.

"Good afternoon, Samuel. How's the king of the wild today?"

He slowly rose and shook his tawny-colored fur and long tufted tail as if he'd just been hosed down.

"I haven't even gotten near you, big guy," Sarah said.

As if in dispute, he roared loudly and she started. The sound reverberated off the hills, and suddenly, other lions housed at the refuge joined in. The noise was a spectacular chorus that could only be described as a feral concert in stereo. She grinned excitedly, absolutely thrilled to witness such a powerful broadcast by so many huge cats.

Samuel, the largest of all the lions, ended his declaration, and Sarah waited until the rest of the roaring died down before continuing to spray the path. In the four years she'd volunteered at the Angeles Crest Wildlife Refuge, the rare and extraordinary symphony of felines had performed only three times. It always made her appreciate the fact that, while Samuel was safely enclosed in their fenced-off and locked areas, he was still the boss. And if anyone questioned that fact, all they had to do was take a gander at the ten-foot-long, muscular powerhouse of a predator whose sharp, retractable claws and powerful jaws would quickly remind them of their inferiority.

Maybe that's why she liked working at the refuge. There, she knew her purpose. She was a caretaker of animals that normally could well take care of themselves, but each one, due to its human-contact experiences, now needed help. Man was responsible for their plight and she could assist. The more powerful the creature, the better she felt, being one who'd grown up thinking she wasn't much, but now caring for these truly magnificent beasts.

"Sarah?"

It was Madeleine Dumont, the owner of the refuge. Since the fires had started around Los Angeles, Sarah hadn't seen much of her. Madeleine was on high alert, keeping in touch with officials in the event one of the fires began to creep, or roar, toward them. Luckily, none were close enough for them to begin evacuation measures. Sarah turned off the hose nozzle. "Yes?"

"Would you help me on fence patrol? I'll pull the Jeep around."

"Of course," she said as she turned toward Samuel, who was now sitting in a patch of sun, eyes closed and head raised to the warmth.

"I'll be back, Sam." And she would. As often as they wanted her to.

Chapter Two

Chris drove up Fuller Street and parked at the end, behind two fire trucks blocking the entrance to Runyon Canyon Park. She'd been to the 160-acre site many times to run and hike. It was conveniently smack-dab in the heart of Hollywood, just north of the strip, and offered not only great trails up to the top of the Hollywood Hills, but breathtaking views of the city. This trip, however, was far from enjoyable. Firefighters were busy running hoses up the trails to catch an errant patch of flames whose originating embers must have been carried by the brown, scorching winds. Several trees were crackling in their death throes, looking like old men with arms flailing in desperation.

"Stay here, Abel," Chris said, and exited the squad car. Burnt and smoldering wood filled her nose, and she swiped at it to ease the sting.

Amid the organized maneuvers of the fire crew, she spotted a few men waving her over.

"Bergstrom," one firefighter said as she approached, "glad it's you."

"Hello, Halloran. Who's your friend?"

About twenty feet away, a tall man, dressed in dirty pants and an equally dirty long-sleeve shirt, crouched with his back against a tree. Strangely, he was sopping wet.

"This guy showed up and started screaming at us."

"You're killing the canyon!" The man flapped his arms wildly. "I'll murder you all!"

"And?" Chris ignored the man.

"He tried to stop us from getting to the fire. He's been grabbing at hoses and pushing my guys, so we called."

"Why's he wet?"

"Turned the hose on him. It was the only way I could keep him away from my guys."

"Good thinking." Chris nodded and stepped closer to the man, who smacked the palms of his hands against his thighs and then stood. "Sir, I don't know what's going on, but we can talk about it."

The man cocked his head as if he'd just heard a dog whistle.

She stepped closer to him, watching for any slight movements that would indicate he was either going to attack or run. "We'll talk about the trees, okay?"

She reached him in two more side steps and put her hand on his shoulder. She continued talking to him because the physical contact seemed to keep him docile.

She ran her hand down his arm. "We all just want to be safe here," she said as she stealthily turned him around and cuffed him.

Patting him down and finding nothing that concerned her, she took him by one arm. "What's your name, sir?"

He mumbled something and began looking around as if he'd just noticed where he was.

Chris nodded to Halloran. "My friend here and I are going to walk over to my car so we can talk."

The man didn't say much that made sense and didn't seem to understand her questions, so she finally propped him against her car. Abel barked ferociously from the backseat, and the man seemed content to stare at him.

She could charge him with assault on an emergency worker

or just call it a 5150 and have him sent to the Cuckoo Plaza Suites for a seventy-two-hour vacation. But he'd disrupted the firemen by getting in their way and making threats. The pungent aroma of beerspiration indicated he was probably drunk as well, so she called dispatch and asked for a transport. Slam dunk. You break the law, you go to jail.

Chris loved the finality and conclusiveness of the law. While the words of the penal codes could be interpreted, following the letter of the law made all the behaviors in life toe a neat and respectable line. Living by this code was as black and white as the colors on her squad car.

After one of her patrol buddies drove the confused man away in his squad car, Chris looked at Abel, who wagged his tail, looking hopeful, and she smiled. Since his built-in kennel took up the entire backseat, he was her guarantee that she'd never have to transport anyone. No puking, peeing, pounding, or just plain stupid talk from bad guys.

Okay, she'd sometimes have to clean up Abel's pee, but it somehow seemed more tolerable than that of the lawbreakers she encountered. And the added bonus? She loved her partner.

❖

Sarah had forgotten to get something for dinner, so she turned into the market parking lot and, surprisingly, found a spot by the front door. Meals with the family were just a little more bearable than an appendectomy without anesthesia, but she had to go. Her sister was getting engaged, so the stage was set for another play in which dear old dad toasted the grand occasion and everyone smiled in feigned unison.

Again, she'd watch the time and hope that no one would say anything that would send her into orbit. Her family was never going to change, and she expected their banter to not only reveal their ignorance about the way people really lived but to piss her the hell off. And every time, she'd coach herself to ignore the remarks, rise above all the ignorance, and just get through the evening. But damned if she wouldn't always feel the sharp slits when her veneer began to crack. As much as she tried to stave off the inevitable, a cascade of frustration would erupt from her gut. And if she was lucky, she'd escape before her anger bubbled up to her mouth.

It would be so easy to dilute her brain with alcohol and deaden the receptacles that took in their diatribe, but that was the easy and obtuse way out. She should know; she'd learned that trick from watching everyone else in her family.

No, in order to pass the night she'd clench and release her fists, do deep breathing, or think of a warm, sunny beach far from everyone.

Her food contribution that night was a salad. The required dish, according to her mother, would be the correct combination of oak-leaf lettuce, a little arugula, a small bit of peppery watercress, chips of pecans, perfectly ripened grape tomatoes, not cherry, in a perfect presentation of a light sprinkling of balsamic vinegar, a splash of soy, salt, pepper, and a little olive oil.

She walked down the aisle of canned goods feeling the tightness that always gripped her stomach. Somehow, God had jettisoned her into the wrong family. Why had she been brought up with them? She hated not liking them and dreaded the searing slices of guilt that constantly raked her heart, but she couldn't make herself feel otherwise.

From childhood, their words and actions, so unenlightened and callous, had seeped into her soul, and not only was she a product of the kind of despicable philosophy that they personified, but it was also one of the ingredients of the shitty stew of education that her parents had raised her to consume.

She usually had two choices, to cave or to fight. She wandered down another aisle, loathing the evening to come because invariably she'd be pushed into one of those choices. Anticipation always made her stomach turn, but tonight, if only in a small way, she'd choose how she wanted to respond before her family forced her into an either/or situation.

❖

One of the conveniences of having Abel was that Chris could take her squad car home every afternoon. After long ten-hour shifts, she didn't have to waste time driving back to the station to change vehicles. Of course, citizens would occasionally flag her down, but one call to dispatch to turn the incident over to another patrol officer and she was on her way again.

But today, she'd helped one of her partners wrestle with a suspect who'd sliced his arms, and by the time they had him under control, her pants and shirt were stained with blood. Luckily she had no cuts and had washed down with soap and water, as well as an alcohol-based hand sanitizer, in case the man had a contagious disease.

She changed out of her vest and button-down shirt after she got home. She left her patrol pants on and threw on a Los Angeles Police Department T-shirt, the kind they used when they worked out at their gym or wore to casual functions. She noticed a small stain below the words BERGSTROM-LAPD K-9 TEAM embroidered on her left chest. Her academy training caused her arm muscles to jerk upward with the intent of ripping off the shirt and finding a perfectly clean one. The Pavlovian urge was strong, but she resisted. Hell, all she had to do was run out to the store. Then no one would bark at her and make her do forty pushups for looking like a shit hole.

She fed Abel and grabbed the keys to her SUV. She would have rather cracked open an ice-cold soda and flopped on the couch, but for the last couple of weeks, her cupboards had been winning a contest against Mother Hubbard.

She parked in the Whole Foods Market lot, the inescapable smoke from the local fires assailing her as she opened the car door. As she entered the store, she rubbed the ashy feeling from her eyes. Mid swipe, she glimpsed a woman dressed in a light-brown, sleeveless ribbed sweater and brown print skirt. From her angle, the woman seemed to be in her early or mid-thirties, with hair a hint lighter than her sweater, resting on her shoulders as regally as a velvet robe on royalty. Chris blinked and she was gone.

Just as well, she thought. Her last girlfriend had cheated on her for so long that when it finally exploded in her face, Chris had been the one who'd felt like the outsider. She'd been the interloper in her own life—the hopeful partygoer without her name on the guest list, the idiot without the password. It was better to just stay out of the romantic ring of fire.

Chris grabbed a hand basket and headed in the opposite direction of the lovely brown sweater, less because she wanted to follow her and more because she had a shopping mission.

"Face it, Bergstrom," she told herself. "You were born divorced. You're better off without the insanity of someone else's life."

In the produce section, she loaded up on greens for the week. She'd cook a whole chicken, wrap the pieces in spinach or lettuce, and then parcel it out over the next few days. It kept well in the small cooler that sat in the passenger's seat and provided quick nourishment between calls.

Now, she needed a tasty snack for her lunches, something that would end the boring reign of bananas she'd been eating the past two weeks and the Pink Lady apples in the weeks prior to that. Rounding the corner, between the cara cara oranges and muscat grapes, she found her nirvana. In a large bin the plumpest, most delectable Oregon blackberries were displayed like juicy, obsidian gems waiting for someone to quarry and consume them.

"Oh, you chubby little delights." Chris swallowed back a sudden hankering.

"Shall I leave you all alone?"

Chris jumped, jerking her hand toward her holster that wasn't there.

In an instant, the brown-sweatered woman stepped back. "I'm sorry I startled you."

"Crap," Chris blurted out as she put her hands up in some sort of embarrassed armistice. "I'm so sorry."

The woman seemed to study her in the same composed manner a pageantry judge would consider a New Year's Day float. Chris was still a little sweaty from the bulletproof vest she'd worn all day, and now she suddenly grew even clammier. The woman was extremely beautiful and perfectly built. Her shoulders were strong but feminine, as were her hips, legs, and arms. While normally Chris would have politely and deferentially ignored her flawlessly shaped breasts, they would've demanded consideration from even a blind person.

The woman read the words on Chris's LAPD T-shirt, taking more time than an art connoisseur would regard a Picasso, and finally said, "I hope I haven't broken any laws, Officer…?"

"Bergstrom. Chris."

"I take it you adore blackberries?"

Chris laughed. "It's June. And it's a short season."

This time the woman laughed and Chris relaxed.

"Well, the way you were looking at them, I wasn't sure I should reach between you and the fruit."

"That intense, huh?"

"Like you hadn't eaten in days."

Chris tore a plastic bag from the roll nearby. "Please, help yourself."

"I'm Sarah, by the way."

They stood side by side as they filled their bags. "Nice to meet you." Unexpectedly, Chris's entire body experienced a confusing mix of calmness and excitement.

"Do you usually come here to accost the produce?"

"Yes. I mean, no. Well, if I must admit, the fruit here is worth stalking, at the very least."

"And what's the charge for that, Officer Bergstrom?"

"Well, it's a violation of penal code 646.9, I believe."

"Doesn't sound too serious."

Chris picked up the fattest berry she could find. "The charge is stalking, and it is to this little guy."

"Are you indicting yourself?"

"Only if this berry decides to press charges."

Sarah plucked the piece of fruit from Chris and popped it in her mouth. Between chews, she said, "I've destroyed the evidence."

"You've killed the witness."

The way Sarah's eyes widened as she raised her hand to her mouth was so adorable Chris swore the manager of the grocery store had just turned up the heat.

"Well, do you suppose you'll have to detain me now, Officer?"

Was this really happening? Was Sarah flirting with her? Did she want something more than just a produce-section chat? Stranger things have happened, she thought. Whether or not Sarah meant anything by her question, Chris could play along. She pulled her pen and small notebook from her front pocket.

"A phone number will suffice for now. That is, until I investigate this case and determine if the charges will stick."

Sarah smiled as if she were about to reveal a secret. She placed both hands over Chris's, paused, and then slipped the pen and notebook from her fingers.

"This," she said as she wrote, "is my cell number. I don't suggest you ask for my license, as you'll find, when you run me, that I have a fondness for speed." She handed the pad and pen back. "I hope that fact doesn't impede your investigation."

A chuckle bubbled up from Chris's throat and she shook her head. Women like Sarah didn't just walk up to her and flirt. Well, not gorgeous women with a wicked wit and amazing eyes, at least.

Pocketing the pen and notepad, she stepped backward. "I'll be in touch."

As she turned to walk away, Sarah said, "Oh, and I also steal those paint stirrers from the hardware store."

Chris laughed and waved at Sarah. She might have needed some other groceries, but the mental list she'd entered the store with was now a blank sheet of paper. At the register, she tried to catch one more glimpse of Sarah, but the cashier scanned her items and took her money too quickly. Chris stopped at the exit to the store. She wanted to call Paige and say, "You're never going to believe what just happened." And it was true, because she almost couldn't have imagined it herself. It was as if she'd just had a lone sighting of a UFO. She wanted someone else to know. She wanted to gush all over Paige about Sarah and retell the details of an event that seemed impossible.

She looked around the parking lot. Where the hell was her car? Her brain couldn't process anything but the thrill of Sarah still reverberating inside her. She actually felt giddy, which wasn't an emotion she often had anything to do with.

How could something as benign as a trip to the store change into an encounter that made her forget where she'd parked not twenty minutes earlier? She fished her keys out of her pocket and clicked the door-unlock button. The chirp answered her question, and she sure as heck hoped no one in the parking lot would think she'd suddenly gone feebleminded.

❖

As the cashier rang up her total, Sarah bagged the ingredients for the family salad. The red apples, white and red grapes, navel oranges, blackberries, and bananas would make her mother's eyeballs spin. The "horribly ordinary" produce was a declaration, though. Fruit was fruit, and to turn a nose up at anything that wasn't exotic and therefore acceptable was bullshit.

Her mother expected the best and then allowed the society of the rich to decide what those things were. Obviously plain old red apples and conventional bananas were unacceptable because they were just too average.

The cashier announced her grocery total, and Sarah sifted through her cash.

And what was so bad about average? She longed to live a regular life where people were just…normal.

Like the woman she'd met at the blackberry bin. She was a normal person, a working cop, who probably didn't care if her oranges came from Florida instead of Venezuela.

However, Sarah thought as the cashier handed her some change, the cop was refreshingly far from average. Her short-cropped, thick head of brown hair, lightly dusted with gray, the no-nonsense olive-green eyes, and her strong, chiseled jawline added up to a striking combination of beauty and strength. And she was able to match jocularities with her. It was silly to say they clicked, but they had. A box of popcorn and a dose of butter didn't complement each other more naturally than she and Chris did.

Her day was definitely turning around. She'd driven to the store dreading the upcoming dinner, but now she marveled at the fortunate turn of events. Of the thousands of people that walked in and out of Whole Foods, Sarah had been lucky enough to pick the perfect day and time to chance upon a woman who could awaken every cell in her body and infuse lightness and joy in places that had been starved of those pleasures for too damn long.

A marvelous feeling of weightlessness overcame her, and she would never have dreamed its impetus would come in the form of a uniformed police officer.

Whole Foods had just become Sarah's favorite store.

She took the grocery bag containing the ingredients of her "fuck you" salad and headed toward the store's automatic doors, happy to be minutes away from pissing her mom off, but much happier to have met one Officer Bergstrom.

❖

All day Saturday, the winds blew through the hills and the firemen chased the flames as they would a killdeer, the spry little bird that fakes her injuries to drive predators away from her nest but stays just out of reach.

Chris had lost count of how many acres had been reported burned and how many houses had been lost. The strangeness of the ochre-tinged day and the charred smells of wood and brush created an eerie ambiance throughout a city that was usually a little too bright and quite full of the spicy smells of ethnic foods and the metallic, oily tang of smog.

At noon, Chris pulled her squad car into the station and let Abel out. It was just under one hundred degrees, and the thick, burnt-smelling air assaulted her like a cheap blow-dryer.

"Take a break," she said, and he dutifully trotted to a patch of grass and peed. She put him back in the car, engine and air conditioner running, and went inside.

"Hey, Bergy, how's your partner?"

"Bored, actually," she said to one of her buddies, a tall young man named Cates.

"No bites?"

"Not for a while."

"Maybe it's pilot error."

Chris turned to see Sergeant Shaffer standing in the doorway. He'd never recovered from being kicked off the K-9 team for some questionable bites. When Chris got his spot, he looked for opportunities to undermine her to the rest of the force.

"I'd have to disagree, Sergeant. She found two pounds of meth the other night."

As Shaffer walked away he said, "Not sure a woman can handle the job."

Chris shook her head. "What a dick."

"Hey, nice bust anyway."

She sat down at a bank of computers and punched in her password. Four other officers were sitting around her typing up their reports. Cates, Miles, Forester, and Warshaw had been on the force almost as long as Chris had. They were all really good officers and treated her like one of the guys. Normally, Chris supposed that would be a bad thing, but on the force, lack of gentlemanliness meant equality. She was just as much the brunt of jokes as any other officer, and she'd received her fair share of razzes and pranks. Having more seniority meant that her repertoire of pranks far outnumbered theirs. And they were all very aware that she could deal out the best of the monkeyshine.

The computer's query screen came on, and she logged onto the case-filing page. Hopefully, she'd have a bit of time to write some reports before her next call. She opened her small notebook and flipped a few pages to the most recent notes. She had two domestic-disturbance calls, with names, descriptions, and quotes. On the next page, she had one breaking-and-entering and three car searches to write up. Turning to the next page, she paused. In a different script was Sarah's name and phone number. Below that, it read *the berry killer.*

A child with a new red balloon couldn't have smiled wider than Chris did. Out of nowhere, an incredibly interesting woman had walked up and changed her day. And as unexpectedly as their encounter had begun, its conclusion had been just as unpredictable. In one moment they were talking about fruit, and in the next, Sarah made it known that she was interested enough to give Chris her number. If Sarah could do that, Chris reasoned, then *she* could certainly pick up the phone and dial.

After a few rings, she heard the same voice and felt a rush of anticipation.

"Sarah? This is Chris. Officer Bergstrom."

"Ahhh," Sarah said, her voice as smooth as a velvet pillow. "Hello, Officer."

"I was calling to follow up on an incident I witnessed yesterday."

"Yes," she said, and paused before saying, "but, I must inform you that the statute of limitations has run out on *rubus fruticosus* transgressions."

"Rubus…?"

"It means blackberry. I looked it up."

How cute was that?! "Well, you may be correct about berry slaughter, but this state has no limits on first-degree… fruiticide."

Sarah's overly dramatic sigh made Chris want to giggle. She knew the goofy smile she couldn't wipe off her face would raise taunts from her police brethren.

"I suppose I'll need to come in for questioning?"

Chris suppressed a giggle. "Yes, we require that."

"We?"

"Berrrrrrgy!" The heckles started.

She glared at Cates. "We, as in the city of Los Angeles."

"I'll only talk to you."

"Ahhhhhhhhhh, sookie sookie, now!"

She flipped Warshaw a middle finger. "That can easily be arranged."

"When does the city want me?"

"At seventeen hundred hours."

After a long pause Sarah said, "Do I add or subtract two hours…?"

"Five o'clock."

Cates and Warshaw were now singing quite badly. "Yooooou, your sex is on fire."

Chris threw her pen at them. "Any delay, reasonable or not, will be heavily weighed against you."

"Tell me where, then."

"How about Lilly's Coffee Cart?"

"In front of the Laurel Canyon Country Store?"

"Yes."

"Do I need to wrap up my personal affairs before coming?"

"Not yet."

"That's a relief. See you then."

When she heard the phone click off, Chris stared at the computer screen. This was so unlike her, the blatant flirting and forward behavior. Things like this were supposed to go in a logical, sequential order. People were supposed to start by chatting and getting to know each other over a period of time and, eventually, request a date. By then, both parties would know each other rather well and things would naturally progress.

A few empty cups got thrown her way.

"You guys are assholes."

They laughed and turned back to their computers.

She was about to meet up with a mystery woman whom she'd spent only five minutes with in the produce section of a grocery store. All she knew was her name. What kind of person would she turn out to be? Could she be a uniform groupie? That fetish was pretty popular, and she'd seen her share of loony Lulus, but they were usually pretty obvious. What little she knew of Sarah, she liked. Her humor and wit were just as attractive as her sexy face and body. But she might be too good to be true.

The only way she'd find out for sure was to meet her. She was throwing caution into a wood chipper to get sliced up and disseminated into an explosion of scattered and unrecoverable guts. And it felt great.

❖

"Get outta here," Paige Cornish said. "This isn't like you at all."

Chris had just left a call on Melrose Avenue and was heading up Fairfax. "I know, right?"

"You just met her yesterday and you've got a date tonight?"

"This evening, actually. Five o'clock."

"You're usually so by the book. This is reaching out of your comfort zone."

"I know, and you're not making it any easier."

"Five o'clock, huh? That doesn't give you much time to get Abel home and shower."

"Like I said." Chris fidgeted with the stitching on her steering wheel. "Not helping. Anyway, yeah, I figured it also wouldn't give me much time to get nervous."

"You'll be fine, my friend. It's been a while, but that's just because you're picky."

"I might be picky, but I sure didn't think I was reckless."

"Just because you met her at Whole Foods?"

"No, because we were flirting within, like, five seconds."

"What's wrong with that? Sometimes crazy things happen."

"To you, Paige. You're the one who spends your days on exciting movie sets and sees the insane celebrity stuff that happens. You're the one who dabbles in the lives of the rich. You met a famous actress, for God sakes, and fell in love. You marched right in there and swept Avalon Randolph off her feet. I mean, who has the balls to go after the most popular actress in Hollywood? Or, for that matter, to go after anything with that much confidence? Not me. I don't do those things."

"Maybe you should. You've been single since your ex decided to cheat on you in a massively royal fashion. It's natural that you've been kind of sequestered, but I'm glad you met this woman. Besides, being all safe and orderly hasn't gotten you too far lately."

"I was raised to do things by the book, Paige. That's my comfort zone. This…I don't even know her!"

Paige whispered into the phone like she was narrating a horror movie. "Getting to know her is how it starts."

"Now you're freaking me out. I have no idea who she is, where she lives, or what she does for a living. She could be a 5150 or a serial killer or something."

"So, take your gun."

"Paige…"

"Is your Spidey sense going nuts?"

"A little."

"Chris, chill out, really. It might not be about her. It might be that your own disciplined head is in higgledy-piggledy chaos."

"Thanks."

"Listen to me. You're going on a date, not a domestic-violence call. You'll be fine. I'm sure she's nice and you'll have a great time. And if you don't, it was just one date. No harm, no foul."

As Chris turned north on La Brea Avenue, her radio squawked. "I gotta go, Paige."

"Did that help?" It was Paige's favorite sign-off.

And Chris always replied in kind. "No."

CHAPTER THREE

With Abel safely secured in the backyard kennel and his mister on, Chris showered quickly and was parking close to the Canyon Country Store with five minutes to spare. As she walked up Kirkwood Street, she automatically put her hand into the pocket that carried her cell phone. She checked its presence out of habit in case someone was texting to say they were running late or needed directions.

Clicking on her recent calls she suddenly realized she didn't even know Sarah's last name. It felt a little reckless to agree to meet someone who was effectively a complete stranger. What if her last name was Dahmer or Manson? If she thought about it too long she'd worry that, much like a tightrope walker staring at the absence of a net below, this might not be a good sign.

Looking toward the sky, she tracked where the smoke was darker in some areas than others, just to see where she was in relation to the hot spots. Though Laurel Canyon wasn't threatened by any immediate danger, it was still a canyon. Angelinos knew these areas could be subject to increased winds and, because of their tight geographical shape, temperature inversions, which rapidly accelerated the travel of fire.

She'd heard too many stories of people caught in canyon fires. But the worst she'd deal with today were irritated eyes.

Sarah was standing beside Lilly's Coffee Cart when Chris

rounded the corner. She wore tight jeans with white threading and a white peasant top. Chris loved the more casual look as much as the sweater and skirt. When Sarah turned and smiled at her, all of Chris's concerns dropped to the sidewalk and she quickly stepped past them.

The cart sat in front of the Canyon Country Store, a historical building that had served the locals since 1929. Tucked up under a wide awning, the cart was designed to look like a gypsy caravan, with a canvas roof stretched over curved wooden frames and elaborately carved and painted trim along the top and sides. They ordered iced cappuccinos and sat at a table so diminutive their knees touched. She flashed back to the first time she saw Sarah walking through the store, and a buzz of exhilaration swept through her because they were this close now.

"These fires are crazy," Sarah said. "This is the worst season I've seen."

"Yeah, it's pretty bad. This heat isn't helping at all. I hope the winds die down and they're able to get control."

A moment of silence fell on them. Chris thought Sarah's expression was warm with amusement or something like that, but she was nervous as hell inside. Blackberries were the only thing they had in common so far.

"When I mentioned Lilly's," Chris said, hoping to quell the quiet, "I was glad you knew about it."

"I come up here every so often. It's such a great neighborhood." Sarah looked around and then pointed. "Did you know Jim Morrison and Pam Courson lived right there? At 8021 Rothdell Trail."

"I knew they lived close by and that he wrote 'Love Street' about their place."

"I adore everything about the counterculture movement of the sixties. This area was, like, Los Angeles's answer to Haight-Ashbury in San Francisco."

Chris nodded and the tendrils of her nervousness began to

recede. "Joni Mitchell and Dave Crosby hung out here, too, I understand."

"I don't smoke pot or anything," Sarah said. "I mean, I love the hippie culture, but I don't want you to be uncomfortable. I mean, you're a cop."

"Oh." Chris finally understood the segue. "Thanks. Yeah. I'm not too keen about drugs."

"I did have my wild phase, I suppose."

"When you were younger?"

Sarah nodded. "Didn't we all?"

"I didn't." When Sarah's expression turned into a dubious gaze, Chris said, "My parents were both in the military. My father retired early and then served ten years at my station as a sergeant. So I grew up in a very strict house. There was good and bad, right and wrong. That was it. And drugs, of course, were wrong."

"Didn't you rebel?"

Chris thought a moment. Why would she rebel when her whole childhood had been about garnering her parents' approval? If she walked the narrow line of obedience, she got infrequent praise. Hugs and kisses, things she saw her friends receive, were out of the question.

"I guess," she said, mentally fast-forwarding to her teen years, "they thought my being gay was a pretty serious rebellion. But when I joined the police force, my father was already there and watched my every move."

"Is he still there?"

"No, he retired a few years ago. But he keeps in touch with all the guys, which is a pain in the ass. It feels like he still has me in his bead."

"Bead, as in bead of a gun sight. I get it. Cop humor, huh?"

"Yeah." Chris smiled. "Where did you grow up? And, for that matter, where do you live now?"

"I grew up not too far from here. Now I'm on Holly Oak Drive."

"I know where that is. Under the Hollywood sign, right?"

"Pretty much, yeah, but it's a hell of a hike."

Chris laughed. The altitude change between Sarah's neighborhood and the sign was about nine hundred feet, almost straight up.

"Did you grow up around here?"

Sarah sipped her coffee before answering. "Yeah. I'm a native. You?"

"Raised at Camp Pendleton. My mom and dad are Marines. Retired, now. They live in El Toro, and I moved far away the very second I graduated from high school."

"Your holiday gatherings must be as fun as mine."

"I don't know. Mine were drinks at exactly seventeen hundred hours followed by dinner at eighteen hundred hours, with a mandatory disappearance of children at nineteen hundred hours."

"You might have mine beat. The drinks part was the same, but usually everything went to shit after that because everyone was falling over or fighting."

"I believe you might have won the fun contest." Chris liked Sarah's wit. She seemed genuinely real and sincere. "What do you do for a living?"

"I don't work."

There was a pause, which piqued Chris's interest. She'd seen that look before in people she'd questioned on the street. While she didn't believe Sarah was concocting a lie, she was definitely doing some careful word-selecting.

Sarah looked straight into Chris's eyes, as if she was waiting for the slightest of clues in Chris's expression. "I'm a trust-fund baby."

That was a surprise. Chris's only point of reference were the few reality TV shows where the sight of hordes of shoes, lots of drama, and snotty attitudes made her change channels faster than when she clicked over to swamp pig fighters and repo bounty spectacles. She wasn't sure how to respond so she said, "You don't look like a trust-fund baby."

Sarah chuckled. "I try not to revel in it. I do a lot of volunteering and keep to myself a lot."

"So I won't be seeing you out at the clubs with anyone whose last name is a hotel chain?"

"No!" Sarah almost spit out her coffee, but it still seeped out of her mouth and down her chin.

Chris began to reach up with her thumb to catch the drops and suddenly clenched her fist. She wasn't used to involuntary reactions, especially when they were intimate, and especially when they involved someone she'd just met. But Sarah's unexpected dribble was so adorable, the urge to touch her, to make a connection, was intense.

"Hey," Chris said, to buy time to sort out that impulse. "Wanna take a walk?"

"I'd love to."

They got coffee refills and headed up Rothdell Trail.

"What kind of volunteer work do you do?" Chris said as they passed Jim Morrison's old house with its unassuming brown exterior and brilliant magenta-flowered bougainvillea spilling over the high, brown walls like foam from a root-beer bottle.

"I work with animals, mostly. In a wildlife-rescue place up in the hills off Mulholland."

"I've called them a few times because of some injured animal calls."

"Really? I've never seen your squad car pull up."

"I don't go there. I just call them to make a pickup. But I'd like to see it."

Sarah turned to her with a crooked smile that Chris imagined could mean a lot of different things.

"I'd love to give you a tour," she said. "Do you like animals?"

"I'd better. I'm a K9 officer."

Sarah stopped walking. "You are? Why didn't I know that when I met you?"

"Because he gets a bath quite often."

"No. I mean I didn't see it on your shirt."

"It was there."

"Where?"

"Left chest, below my name."

"The blackberries must have temporarily stymied my skills of observation."

"Yeah, that must have been it."

"What's your dog's name?"

"Abel."

"He's your partner?"

"Badge and all."

"I'd like to meet him."

"If I get a tour of the rescue facility, then you can meet Abel. Deal?"

"Absolutely."

As they turned right onto a back street, Chris felt happier than she usually did on a first date. The ease of their talking was a delightful change from the nervous and choppy exchanges she usually had in similar situations. Those conversations were usually more difficult to keep alive than the flicker of a candle in a windstorm.

"You're easy to talk to."

"I like that about you, too." Sarah bumped Chris's shoulder with her own.

"Sarah, what's your last name?"

"You're going to run me, aren't you?"

"I may," she said, trying to look serious, though she felt so energized, she wanted to giggle.

"Pullman," she said. "It's German, I think, and it means 'bottle blower' or something like that."

"Bottle blower, huh?"

"Exciting, I know."

"Bergstrom, my last name, means 'mountain stream' in Swedish. I just got a travel-brochure picture for a name, and you got a cool occupation."

"I suppose 'mountain stream' is better than 'littered alleyway.'" Her impish grin pulled her eyes into a very cute squint.

This time, Chris did giggle. "You do have a way of looking at the positive."

Sarah turned to her with a bright face. "How'd you guess my middle name?"

"Sarah, the optimistic bottle blower. I like it."

"What's your middle name?"

"It's after my Asian grandfather, Pee Yee Yinda."

Sarah hesitated and then narrowed her eyes. "Chris peeing in the mountain stream. Nice."

"Well, I've never been, but I hear China's a great place."

"It is," Sarah said.

"You've been there?"

"Once, when I was a teenager. I raised money in high school to go. A group of us went. My best friend, Natalie, and I sold chocolate. Can you believe that?"

"Those bars with almonds?"

"Yes!"

"I love them."

"We wanted to get enough money to pay for our trip and give a donation to a children's abuse shelter in Hollywood. We sold that chocolate to everyone we could find."

"So, China was great?"

"Yeah. We spent a week in Shanghai and got tattoos."

"You did?"

Sarah pulled up her left sleeve. A beautiful group of Mandarin characters wrapped around her shoulder. The ink was dark purple, which made it seem softer.

"What does it mean?"

"Even in hell, angels can find you."

"Wow. That's pretty profound."

Her reaction seemed delayed, like she had to bite her lip. Chris wondered what the impetus of the tattoo had been. Whatever secret seemed poised on Sarah's lips, it didn't seem like she wanted to share, so Chris didn't ask.

"What else did you do in Shanghai?"

"Oh, there was more to do than we had time. But we did go to the park called Fuxing. It's got paths and trees, and in this one area couples, like they're on lunch break, are dancing to a loud radio in this round courtyard, and benches and benches of old women in pajamas are belting out Chinese opera. It's amazing.

"And we also spent a day on Dongtai Road, where they have this incredible antique flea market. Streets of stuff, but if you go just a few blocks east, you'll find a plant and animal market. A local told us about the cricket fights, and we went to one."

"Cricket fighting. Are you serious? Is that like dog fighting?"

"No, not at all. The crickets don't get hurt. They just get pissed off at each other, and the first one that backs off is the loser. They fight according to their weight class, and a championship match can have many, many bouts."

"I think you're pulling my leg."

"No, I'm not! People spend millions and millions of dollars on cricket breeding and housing. They even have funerals for the champions. Crickets, as I found out, have been a big part of Chinese culture for centuries. They're considered good luck around the home. And if there's a swarm of them, it means you're supposed to gain wealth."

"You and Natalie like to go off the beaten path when you travel, huh?"

"I just really like the different and diverse parts of our world. Plus, it's a lot more fun to see and do things that the normal tourist doesn't even know about. Even here in L.A., I avoid the touristy areas, which is hard, but the most entertaining stuff isn't where you'd expect it. And I can tell you that you won't see me on

Hollywood Boulevard taking friends to see Grauman's Chinese Theater."

"Because there's no cricket fighting?"

It tickled Chris that Sarah's laugh was so immediate.

"Hey, look." Chris pointed when they'd reached a small T-junction. The street sign read HAPPY LANE. It was a short road of houses that, with characteristic Los Angeles intention, were completely hidden from the street below and comfortably nestled like baby sparrows in a big woodsy nest.

Sarah said what Chris was thinking. "What a great name for a street."

They stopped and looked around. The air was so fresh the L.A. smog must not have known about this little neighborhood. From higher up, a breeze whistled down through the hills, and the California bay laurel trees around them seemed pleased because their leaves looked like they were all clapping.

Then Chris felt Sarah's hand slide into hers. She meant to be a little more discreet but instead looked down in surprise.

A confident grin spread across Sarah's beautiful face. "This…being here with you…feels nice."

Though usually Chris would never do something like this, so quickly, so early on, holding hands seemed exceptionally straightforward and right. And though this wasn't on her normal timeline of the typical dating ritual, it was exciting and calming at the same time. Chris's chest swirled with the flush of their touch while her stomach relaxed to the calming gesture. Chris marveled that, to her, a first date was about seeing what future steps to take while being shaped by past encounters, yet Sarah was quite impressively in the here and now.

Chris squeezed Sarah's hand as they turned to walk back and wondered if this might be the start of something special.

When they got back to Lilly's Coffee Cart, Chris said, "May I walk you to your car?"

"How about I walk you to yours?"

"Okay."

"But here's the challenge," Sarah said. "If I can guess which car is yours, then you have to kiss me."

Well, that was an unexpected twist. Holding hands and now a possible kiss? She only had a moment to think, or she'd be sure to appear somewhat of a drip. Ah, hell.

"If you're that good, you deserve a kiss."

"Just point in the general direction."

Chris did and they began walking.

"What if you don't guess correctly?" Chris said when they were nearing the street she'd parked on.

"Oh, that won't happen. I'm good at this."

Surprisingly, Sarah turned the right direction on Kirkwood Street.

"The BMW's not yours. Too stuffy. That Tesla isn't yours either."

"Why don't you think I could own that Tesla?"

"Because it's mine."

Chris looked back at it. Five-Robert-Tango-Alpha-One-Two-Seven, she read to herself out of habit. The plate was standard issue, not personalized like most of the higher-end cars she pulled over.

They walked a little farther.

"Hmmm, the pickup truck might be yours, but…I don't think so."

"Why?"

"I'm concentrating."

Chris laughed. "Sorry."

Passing three more cars, Sarah said, "No. No. And no." And then she stopped, pointed, and said, "That's the one. The Frontier SUV. That's yours."

"How in the world…how'd you figure it out?"

"The powers of logical deduction."

"That's crazy! I mean, really, how'd you do that? You should apply for the detective position at the police department."

Sarah turned to face her. "I think you should shut up and let me collect."

Chris leaned toward her and they kissed. Their coming together was, alternatingly, yielding and insistent. The gentle softness of Sarah's lips played with the fervid firmness of Chris's tongue and accelerated her heartbeat faster than a hummingbird's. She tasted the earthy trace of cappuccino mixed with, possibly, spearmint gum.

Much too quickly, Sarah pulled away. Her eyes were half open, as if waking from a happy dream.

"Wow," Chris said.

Sarah reached up and cupped Chris's face, drawing her thumb softly over her lips. "I liked that."

"That kiss was as fantastic as your car-finding ability."

"I hope it was better than that," Sarah said as she squinted charmingly, "because I saw you drive away from Whole Foods Market yesterday."

They laughed and fell into a hug. They fit so damn well, a shiver of passion started rising from Chris's legs to her belly. She almost shook her head to remind herself to slow down, but she was having too much fun.

❖

All the way home, Sarah thought about Chris. She was amazing and carried herself with such confidence and control. Maybe a little too much control, if she was to speculate beyond what she'd seen.

But nothing seemed wrong about being with her. She was strikingly good looking and projected an unmistakable sexy vibe that she herself probably wasn't even aware of. Chris understood her sense of humor and also made her laugh. Sarah even tried to walk slower so they wouldn't get back to their cars as fast.

She pulled into the driveway of her home in the Hollywood

Hills, rehashing bits and pieces of their conversation. Their bantering back and forth about the sixties and the origins of their names was a joy that couldn't be topped, even if you put it up against Christmas and puppies.

But one thing bothered her. What did Chris think about the fact that she didn't actually have a job? She used her time well by volunteering, but she wasn't establishing a career or truly living on her own.

Sometimes she hated her birthright. She often dreamt of breaking away from her family and setting off on her own. She could become anything she wanted, to hell with any financial strings that bound her. But the fears and cowardice that forced their way into her head and beat the shit out of the little independent and adventurous spirit inside her would soon douse that notion.

She walked up her porch stairs and unlocked the front door.

Chris seemed self-sufficient and hard working. She was sure Chris had earned anything she had. Normally most everyone did; they graduated from school, got a job, and started building their life.

Sarah had been born into the exception, though. She despised names like "deep pockets," "high baller," "loaded," "friends of the Benjamins"…all the terms that continuously taunted her as badly as the daily jibes of a schoolyard bully. But in all her turmoil, she kept quiet because no one would ever show her any sympathy for being frustrated and unhappy about her family's affluence.

She stood in the foyer and scanned the interior of the house. This all was hers, but it wasn't hers. She hadn't earned a penny toward its purchase price. How had she let this way of life all happen? Why hadn't she rebelled when she was younger and more able to take risks? Long gone were the days of running away from home. She was a cow in a stockyard, not questioning the march that led to the big, ominous building where humans had smiles as strange looking as their menacing tools.

Independence wasn't a virtue she could call her own. And if she didn't respect herself, how would someone like Chris?

And did Chris see those things in her? Did she wonder about the logic of pursuing a woman who constantly chipped her tooth on a silver spoon? Would Chris call again?

She sat down on her couch and put her feet up on the coffee table, marveling that her short time with Chris had made her forget about everything but their togetherness. Chris seemed truly interested in her without knowing much about her life. At the same time, Sarah was excited about getting to know Chris but frightened about Chris getting to know her.

Still, she felt drawn to this new person in her life in extraordinary ways that ran deeper than anybody she'd ever been with, and that made her feel better than anything she could imagine.

❖

Sunday morning came a little too early. Sarah hadn't slept much because she'd spent the night with more energy than she could contain. Her date with Chris had been an unexpected leap forward and out of the stagnant dating puddle she'd been mired in.

Finally she'd found someone who was cute and funny and kind. Chris seemed stable and responsible. Plus, she'd felt so good when they kissed.

From the moment Chris had reacted with such kind understanding to Sarah's silver-spoon admission, she'd wanted to kiss her. Chris didn't show any signs of feigning acceptance of the fact that she didn't have a career or hoping she might share some of her wealth.

The information had passed Chris by as insignificantly as a gnat through a window screen.

But would that impression last? People divulged a lot of

trivial personal information that skipped along the surface during a first date. But later the reality of deeper knowledge could potentially sink her to the bottom.

Sarah had tried to lie down to sleep, but thoughts of inadequacy buzzed around her head like bees trapped in a phone booth. She finally got up and made coffee. When she turned on her laptop to empty her mind, she couldn't resist searching the Internet for Chris Bergstrom. One link led her to an article about Chris's work with Abel. It talked about their training and Abel's ability to detect drugs and people. It also noted the rarity of a female K9 officer and touted awards they'd received. The attached picture of Chris in her uniform was impressive. Sarah didn't think of herself as having a thing for uniforms, but she might consider it now.

She found a few pictures of Chris on different web pages, mostly illustrating articles about her police work. And she uncovered one mention of a Chris Bergstrom who contributed to a charity for military children. That had to be her.

They'd parted the day before without any discussion about a second date. She so deeply hoped Chris wanted to see her again. Picking up her cell phone, she realized it was six thirty in the morning. As much as she wanted to call Chris, she resisted what might be an inappropriate gesture so soon after meeting her. Instead, she showered and left for the wildlife refuge.

"You're early," Allan said to Sarah as she walked up the path toward him. He was standing by the baboon enclosure, his hands in an electrical box.

"What're you doing?"

"The sensor for the light is out. Sasha and her family, here, have been in the dark for two nights."

Sasha, the matriarch of her tribe of Guinea baboons, sat nearby and watched them with interest. She lifted her long dog-like muzzle and sniffed the air when Sarah approached. Seemingly satisfied, she closed her eyes and lazily scratched her hip. A few other baboons, namely Billy, Tessa, and Pudge, slowly walked over, a breeze coming from the top of the hills behind them riffling their manes.

"Maybe they like being in the dark. It'd feel more like their original habitat."

"Maybe for the young ones," he said, nodding to Billy, Tessa and Pudge. "But the furry old lady was raised in captivity, and she likes having sort of a night-light."

Sadness spread throughout Sarah like syrupy melancholy that wouldn't easily dissipate. And she knew why. Sasha had never had a normal childhood. And neither had she.

CHAPTER FOUR

Abel's bark woke Chris up. He announced an approaching dog and warned of a human in distinctly different ways. This was the latter, so she got up to investigate who was close by.

In boxers and a T-shirt, she trotted toward the front of the house. The doorbell rang and she glanced at her wall clock. It was just after eight a.m.

Chris's neighbor, Mrs. Richards, started talking as soon as she opened the door.

"Chris, honey, could you bring Abel over? We have a situation."

"What's the problem, Mrs. Richards?"

"It's those children next door again. They're so loud, and I think they throw themselves against the wall just to make noise. Their mother is there, but she won't do anything about it."

Elderly Mrs. Richards lived in the apartment building next door and managed to come by asking for police assistance at least once a month.

"Have you talked to the mother?"

"Oh. No. She won't listen anyway. I mean, she never responds to my notes, so I doubt she'd talk to me."

"How many notes did you leave?"

"Maybe eight or ten. So I need you to bring Abel. Just the sight of him will get her attention."

"Mrs. Richards, I can't bring Abel over. This is a personal

matter, and it doesn't appear that anyone is breaking the law. If you really feel that the noise is too loud, you can call the police."

"But you are the police."

"I'm not working right now."

Mrs. Richard's eye's darted back and forth, and Chris almost looked forward to the next thing out of her mouth.

"Can I just borrow Abel, then?"

Chris tried not to laugh. "Abel is a little too much firepower."

The old woman pumped her bicep. "I'm strong."

"I'm the only one who's allowed to handle him."

"Oh." She seemed puzzled. "Well, then. I guess I have to listen to that racket."

"The police are there if you need them, Mrs. Richards."

Chris closed the door and wondered if she should have purchased this house, given that the apartment building was a little too close by. But then again, she was glad she'd decided on the old bungalow. It was perfectly located on palm-lined Palm Street, between Santa Monica Boulevard and Sunset Boulevard, in the gay heart of West Hollywood, and she loved its cheerful exterior personality of light-blue paint and chocolate trim.

She went out to her well-established but slightly overgrown yard and let Abel out of his locked kennel. As usual, though he'd spent all night holding his pee, he was much more interested in playing ball with her.

"Take a break," she said, and he immediately responded to her command, trotting over to lift a leg at a tree.

Chris stood on her brick walkway, her bare feet cool on the red clay blocks, and waited until he was done. He was then back on task and brought his favorite ball to her, dropping it at her feet. She threw it, always careful to avoid a high lob. If it bounced wrong and went over the fence, Abel would immediately follow.

The Zen-like repetition of ball-throwing allowed her to reflect upon Sarah and their date. The walk had been perfect. The conversation was truly pleasurable. And their amazing kiss had been a definite surprise.

She'd call her again, she was sure. Chris very much wanted to find out more about the woman she'd encountered over blackberries.

❖

Sarah sat on her living-room couch, reading a novel about vampires in modern-day Paris. Since childhood, literature had provided a distraction from a family who was overly concerned with superficial endeavors that rankled her. They spent too much time and energy fussing about how they should look and act, which, even to her immature mind, seemed shallow. They were trying to conceal who they really were, and the amount of energy they expended could have built the pyramids. She hadn't even reached the point of using two hands to count her age when she figured out that family secrets were just that, and breaking the silence was tantamount to treason. And though, at that age, she didn't know what the word "treason" meant, she knew her parents were formidable rulers in the kingdom of what she'd later understand as protocol.

The constant tension made her want to hide in her closet, but decorum required her to at least be in the presence of the people who created her and the other two offspring that had come along, one before and one after her.

Reading seemed to be the most acceptable pastime, her parents ostensibly happy that she was educating herself instead of watching TV.

Now, as an adult, she could spend hours nose-deep in a book, which helped quiet her mind from the tape recordings her parents must have surgically implanted in her brain.

Good girls don't run through the house.

We aren't supposed to raise our voices, are we?
Why can't you be someone we can be proud of?

Books were her sanctuary, and their pages, salvation.

The dull buzz of her cell phone came from the kitchen, so she got up to fetch it.

"Hello?"

"Sarah," came the voice. "It's Chris."

A sudden injection of elation raced through her veins, and she dropped her head back, completely delighted. "Well, hello. How are you?"

"Very well," Chris said. "Happy Sunday."

And it was, now. "Happy Sunday to you."

"I'm calling because I really would," she stretched her words out like a jeweler selling the important aspects of a rare gem would, "like to have a second date with the woman who came from bottle blowers."

"I'd love to. But I must warn you," Sarah said as she sat back down on her couch, "that we blowers of the bottle are a quirky bunch."

"I get the feeling that I'm now supposed to say, how quirky are you?"

"Well, I'm glad you asked. Traditionally, we're adamant about what happens on the second date. We're pretty good at planning and, I must say, expert at a good time."

"Is it because of all the hot air you're used to blowing?"

"Touché, Officer Bergstrom."

"Whatever you plan will be fine with me."

Chris's voice sounded so warm and sincere, Sarah wanted to pause in confused suspension. With words now catching in her throat and her chest feeling strangely like bursting, it was as if joy and contentment, both very foreign emotions to her, were suddenly making themselves at home. "Would…" she said, hoping her voice remained even, "would you like to come over here for dinner?"

"That sounds great."

"Is six thirty okay with you?"

"Absolutely."

Sarah hung up and stared out her front window. Maybe this was the start of a decrease in book time. She suddenly stood up and looked around her living room. The place needed a thorough scouring. She checked her watch and realized that she had lots of time, but she kangarooed around the room anyway, hopping about with joyful enthusiasm.

❖

After a shower, Chris was listening to the television while she picked out jeans and a light-blue pullover and got dressed.

Two of the three fires that burned in Los Angeles County were sixty percent contained. The other one, moving from the northern part of the Angeles National Forest, was still eating its way through fairly inaccessible areas and, other than some calculated firebreaks, water-dropping planes were the only artillery.

Chris hated that so much land was being destroyed. Of course, nature relied on fire to balance its ecosystems and to revitalize and clear away underbrush, as well as expose fresh soil underneath. And some plants need fire to germinate and reproduce.

But every season, too many knuckleheads lit matches or flicked cigarettes out of car windows in numbers that were much more frequent than those caused by lightning strikes or sparks from rock falls.

It bothered her that animals were currently suffering throughout the county. She just prayed that birds and mammals were evacuating and reptiles were burrowing in their holes or finding ponds and streams in which to hide.

Over the voice of the fire reporter, a rapid *bing-bing-bing* punched through. The heavy thumb on her doorbell told Chris that Paige had come by.

She opened the door, and Paige followed her to the back of the bathroom.

Paige sat on the toilet while Chris combed her wet hair. "I'm on my way to the hiking store. Need anything?"

"No, I'm good."

"What are you doing on your day off?"

"I've got a date."

"With the grocery-store lady?"

"Her name's Sarah."

"Slow down, Turbo. Back up a few steps. How'd the date go last night?"

"Really well." Chris watched herself smile in the mirror. "We met in Laurel Canyon, had coffee, and took a walk."

"That's nice."

"She kissed me."

Paige leaned back and crossed her legs, looking like a psychologist analyzing a patient. All she needed was a pipe to chew on. "While that would normally be an ordinary act on the first date, I do know, in your case, that's a big thing. What happened that made you so reckless? Did she put booze in your drink?"

Chris glared at her. "No. It was just a…thing that happened."

"You're not going to get away with that flimsy answer. Kissing on the first date is a whopper for you, I know. You're pragmatic and methodical when it comes to…well, everything."

"I don't know. She's just different. She's so easy to talk to. We have the same sense of humor."

"And she's hot, right?"

She picked up the hair dryer. "Yes, that, too."

"It helps," Paige said. "So if I look at the rampant trend being established here, that means your date tonight will end in sex."

"What?! No!"

"I'm just saying."

"And I'm saying there's no way. A kiss is one thing, but damn, Paige. I'm not that irrational."

"Who says falling into bed is irrational? Love doesn't follow the laws of logic."

"I'm turning my hair dryer on now."

"Crazier things have happened."

"Not to me."

"Don't knock it till—"

"Don't finish that sentence."

"I'm just—"

Chris flicked the dryer switch on. "Not listening."

Paige raised her voice over the noise. "It wouldn't be the end of the world if you got horizontal with grocery lady."

"Sarah. Her name's Sarah. And the chances of that happening tonight are zero."

"Okay." Paige stood. "Got coffee?"

"Yup."

Paige left and Chris tried to focus on the menial task of drying her hair but, instead, grew more and more nervous. What if Sarah tried something like that? Things were supposed to go slowly. That's how the world stayed in control. That's how her heart stayed in control.

❖

Chris followed her GPS toward Sarah's house. Heading toward a cluster of homes nestled in a neighborhood close to the Hollywood sign, she turned onto Holly Oak Drive, a beautiful tree-lined street that was as private as most people could ever wish for. Due to the hills, the houses were only on the upward side of the curvy, ascending street. The other side dropped down to the backyards of the houses below.

She parked at the address she'd been given and took in the house. It was a 1940s home with a classic stucco exterior, painted a stark white that reminded her of island homes in Greece. A short driveway rose upward from the street, meeting a two-car garage, and above it, the first floor was of simple, mid-century modern construction, its conventional windows designed with simple mullions. Typical of most houses in the hills, the steep front yard wouldn't easily accommodate a lawn mower, so it was planted with ivy.

It was a very practical place. Chris liked it immediately.

Chris walked up the steps to the door and cleared her throat. She felt like she'd swallowed sand and chased it with sifted flour. She took a deep breath to calm her nerves.

Sarah answered the door wearing a pink-and-blue-flowered scoop-neck tank top over white jeans. Chris sighed in relief. Her own jeans and long-sleeved brown tunic tee had been the right choice.

"Hi," Sarah said quickly, and her crooked smile reassured Chris she probably wasn't the only one anxious.

They stood inside the foyer and, after a moment of awkward silence, Sarah said, "A tour. Would you like a tour of my place?"

Post-and-beam ceilings ran throughout the house, and the white paint scheme, which extended inside as well, made the place peaceful. All the rooms were loaded with light from an ample arrangement of windows. The living room flowed into the dining room that connected to the kitchen. A wrap-around deck outside provided the perfect vantage point to take in the gorgeous mature trees and lush hillside.

"And the hallway off the living room leads to the bedrooms," Sarah said when they'd stopped in the kitchen. An appetizing aroma of rosemary greeted her. The oven was on, and covered dishes sat on the counter. Sarah had obviously spent some time preparing for this date.

"So, what would you like to drink?"

"What do you have?"

"Wine, water, whiskey, soda."

"Anything diet is fine."

She opened a cupboard. "I'm sure I have some diet Jim Beam in here somewhere." She turned back to Chris with an impish grin.

There, that look. It was the same one she'd had when they were talking in Laurel Canyon.

Sarah turned toward the refrigerator. "How's a Coke sound?"

"Perfect."

Drinks in hand, Chris followed her into the living room where a long, off-white linen sofa lined the wall opposite a stone-faced fireplace. Sitting down, Chris noticed two leather armchairs on either side of the room. A few books were stacked on the floor by one of them.

"What do you like to read?"

"Anything fiction. That's obviously a very general statement, but I really don't have a certain preference. Right now I'm reading a modern-day vampire story. Next it could be about World War Two, outer space, or the Alaskan mountains. I like it all."

As they talked about books they'd read, Chris relaxed enough to truly enjoy the evening. Never too far from her thoughts was the kiss they'd shared. She watched Sarah's lips as she spoke and began to daydream. What would those arms feel like if they were wrapped tight around her? Were her thighs as strong as they appeared to be? How would she look when she was about to—

"Are you okay?" Sarah asked suddenly.

"Yes, why?"

"You started shaking your head."

She couldn't tell her she'd just scolded herself for libidinous thoughts that centered on Sarah's body. "The diet Jim Beam is going to my head."

Sarah laughed and got up from the sofa. "Well then, we'd better get some food in you. I don't want you blowing past the legal limit."

Chris let out a huge breath when Sarah disappeared into the

kitchen. Get your mind out of her panties, she told herself. One kiss and you're already undressing her.

That thought startled her because it was wrong. They needed to have lots more dates before they ended up in the bedroom.

❖

Sarah took the rosemary chicken out of the oven and checked the temperature. Perfect. Transferring the food to the dining-room table that she'd set earlier, she retrieved a bottle of wine and paused. Chris had asked for a soda earlier. Did that mean she didn't drink? Maybe she should serve water instead.

Would she even like the chicken? She was fairly confident of her summer-slaw salad and home-baked rolls.

Bottle in hand, she walked into the living room. Chris had one of her books opened on her lap. She looked so incredibly sexy just sitting there. A flurry of excited little jolts swirled around her stomach.

"Is this okay?" She held up the wine.

"How about something diet?"

"Darn, I just ran out of zero-calorie Merlot. But I think I have some Diet Cokes."

"Are they from a good year?"

"A little young. Two thousand fourteen, I'm afraid."

"Let's try one anyway. I like to live life on the edge."

Sarah grinned. Dinner would go fine.

❖

Sarah couldn't believe they'd sat and talked until the chicken was cold and the trees outside had been obscured by the darkness that had fallen some time ago. They'd shared stories about crazy things they'd seen in Los Angeles, about the schools they went to, and about interior decorating. She loved hearing about the police academy and told Chris more about the wildlife refuge.

Things were going very well, and the dizzy buzz of delight whirred in her head.

"That's the one thing," Chris was saying, "that I need more of. I have hardly any artwork on my walls. I have photos taken by my best friend, Paige. They're all in black and white so I think I need some color."

Sarah nodded. "When I travel, I always look for pieces by local artists. It's my way of supporting them. Usually, I like unknown artists better than the famous ones. It's really fun to discover someone on a city street or at a neighborhood art fair who's just starting out and proud of their work."

"Do you buy paintings or photographs?"

"Come here, I'll show you."

Sarah took her to the long hallway off the living room. "This is where it all goes. It's kind of like my own newbie gallery."

She turned the light on and was thrilled when Chris took in a breath and said, "Wow." She watched her get close to each one, studying the designs and themes.

"This one," Chris said, pointing to an oil painting of two old women sitting on a park bench, "is really nice. Is it kind of like an Impressionistic painting? I'm not that versed in art history."

"Yes, it is. I really loved it because you can't make out a lot of details, but the artist captured the mood. It's like it tells a whole story about their friendship."

"And what's this one?" She stepped over to the one next to the oil.

"That's an abstract," Sarah said as she moved up behind Chris. "It's called *Kiwi Explosion*."

"That's a perfect title. I can see about twenty different shades of green." Chris backed up and bumped into her. She turned around, quickly saying, "Sorry."

Sarah had automatically reached for Chris's hips to catch

her as she turned, and in that moment, standing so close, Sarah couldn't tell what Chris's eyes were saying.

The look of surprise remained, but Sarah also saw a hint of what looked like either fear or hesitation. Whichever it was, Sarah moved one hand up and caressed the side of Chris's face, to reassure her.

Ever-so-slight glances at Sarah's lips told her that maybe Chris was just a little tentative, so she leaned toward her and kissed her.

Chris's sexy and responsive tongue met hers, and Sarah was certain that any wavering must have just vanished.

Strong hands reached around her and pulled her until they bumped into the wall behind Chris. Every part of Chris's body seemed to complement hers as their hips and chests and legs fit together perfectly. Even their breathing increased in a harmonious concert that played the same rhythmic song of immediacy.

Chris groaned and broke the kiss, resting her head back against the wall. A vein in her neck throbbed quickly, and Sarah eagerly ran her tongue over her warm, pulsing skin.

The intensity of their kisses grew more feverish, and suddenly Chris was pushing off the wall. She drove Sarah backward until they crashed into the other wall, and Sarah felt an incredible gush of wetness between her legs.

She was aroused beyond control now, edging to the precipice of any semblance of restraint. Each time Chris moaned, pinwheels whirled in her chest and then let loose, spinning down toward her hips and between her legs.

Unable to stand any longer, she broke the kiss and led Chris down the hall to her bedroom and over to the bed. There, they began kissing again, and Sarah became hopelessly lost in the way Chris seemed to want to devour her. With both hands, she encircled Chris and grasped her pants, tugging her toward her. They dropped onto the bed without breaking contact. The crisp, clean sheets underneath Sarah felt wintery cool against flesh that burned as hot as the L.A. fires outside.

Without a word between them, she eased Chris's pants off. Chris sat up, quickly pulling off her top, and Sarah reached around to unhook her bra. A profuse urgency filled the air, thick with a demanding hunger that made Sarah grow dizzy and her legs shake.

Chris was removing her clothes, her expression so driven and powerful, Sarah would have jumped off a cliff for her right then.

Chris pulled Sarah down on top of her, and the sudden touch of their exposed bodies made Sarah gasp with pleasure. As if finally taking a breath from a long ocean dive, she'd never felt more alive and satiated.

Sarah found Chris's mouth again, wanting to connect and meld into her. They kissed for a long time, exploring each other with their hands and Sarah finding a few scars on her incredible body. She felt muscles strain and soft, supple skin. Chris's body was like a novel and she read every page, over and over.

Chris's hand massaged Sarah's nipple, drawing it into a tight erection that ached in the most beautiful way. And then Chris's mouth was upon it, sucking and licking, causing the ache to travel down, between her legs, and grow there like an oncoming storm. And as a captain responds to the demands of the sea, Chris lowered herself between Sarah's legs and, suddenly, Sarah gasped loudly.

Chris's mouth was doing things Sarah hadn't felt before. Some incredible, hypnotic movements of her tongue and lips sent Sarah spinning uncontrollably toward orgasm.

She clutched Chris's shoulders, reeling from the sensations of Chris between her legs and that luscious mouth consuming her. She was reduced to nothing but the feel of her own lower lips, hot and swollen against Chris's mouth, and then, suddenly, the beautiful tension reached its threshold, exploding with an exquisite release. Sarah screamed out a primal roar that rose and fell with the rhythm that was completely overtaking her.

Chris held on tight as Sarah clutched her, writhing and

bucking from the powerful grip of her orgasm. She came close to passing out and didn't care. Something so incredible was happening, and she would give in to it no matter what.

As the spasms subsided, she felt Chris stroke her stomach and they lay there, suspended in a moment of extreme satisfaction.

Chris moved up the length of her body and Sarah caught her face in her hands, kissing her deeply. The feel of Chris's strong arms wrapped around her brought her back to Earth, and when Chris buried her face in Sarah's neck, she wrapped her arms around her, squeezing as hard as she could.

"My God," she whispered, still breathing in slow heaves. "That…that…was amazing."

"Mmmm," Chris mumbled into her neck and then rolled to her side.

"I've never been that loud. I hope I didn't scare you."

"Not even a little." Chris's eyes were dreamy half slits.

"I had no idea what the 'serve' part of 'protect and serve' meant with you cops."

Chris laughed and shook her head. "You're touched."

"You're just now finding that out?"

Chris turned onto her back, lying hip to hip with Sarah. They looked toward the ceiling, and Sarah was reminded of children witnessing the awe of the nighttime stars.

"I hope you know I had no intention of ending up here. I truly was just showing you my artwork."

"I didn't expect this either."

Sarah found Chris's hand and squeezed. "It was wonderful."

From somewhere up in the hills, a coyote yipped and was answered by another farther away. Other noises from outside came back into focus—leaves tangling in the breeze, the melodious bells of a wind chime.

"I can't stay the night," Chris said after a while.

They both sat up and Sarah reached for her top. "It's okay."

It took a moment to find and then sort their clothes. They

stood next to each other, and Chris looked over to her, smiling, as she turned her top right side out.

As they dressed in silence, a bothersome thought pestered Sarah, and she fought to ignore it. She wouldn't react to what felt like a sudden departure by Chris. She had to have a good reason, she told herself.

As Sarah straightened her hair, Chris put her arms around her. She looked into Sarah's eyes with an attentiveness that calmed her immediately.

"Tonight was wonderful," Chris said.

They kissed, and this time it carried the gentle message that comes after a cherished evening, like a tender "sincerely yours" at the end of a letter.

CHAPTER FIVE

Chris scrolled down the backlog of calls on her monitor and sighed. Normally, she was off from Sunday through Tuesday, but she'd asked to work that morning to avoid climbing the walls at home. Because she was one of only two K9 officers at her station, the lieutenant easily granted her request. But as much as she'd originally hoped a busy day would occupy her mind, it just ended up being a blur of chores that required a lot of mental acuity, of which she had none.

It was dangerous to answer police calls with a mind as absent as a politician's promise. Most of the calls she'd answered had been mundane, largely people squabbling or reports of break-ins. If a serious call came in, she hoped to hell she'd be able to think clearly.

As soon as she'd gotten home from being with Sarah, a torrential monsoon of guilt poured down on her. What the hell had she done? Why had she so quickly fallen into bed with Sarah? Certainly, something primal had taken over in the hall—a force stronger than anything she'd ever experienced or ever thought could be possible. She'd been aware of her actions and a lone voice from somewhere in the back of her mind, telling her to stop. But she hadn't. She'd lost control and made decisions based solely on her body's needs.

That was so not who she was.

Her squad car was parked in back of a convenience store,

which was good, because she needed to close her eyes for a moment and try to get rid of a hangover-sized headache of self-reproach and contrition. She laid her head back and even rubbed it roughly, but nothing was working. Her body wasn't in agreement with her head. She could still feel the weight of Sarah's body on hers. The feel of her soft, warm skin was so intoxicating, she could have sworn she'd been high on something.

And even now, Chris's uniform pants felt too tight. She couldn't still be swollen after this many hours, but she was stimulated. Her desire was so surprisingly fervent that if Sarah suddenly walked up to the squad car, Chris would pull her inside, turn off the radio, and surrender to anything she wanted to do.

And sex in her squad car was absolutely, unquestionably, seriously wrong. It scared her that she felt unable to resist Sarah. One stupid, irresponsible act like that and she could lose her career. The way she'd so easily imagined breaking the rules made her no different than an addict looking for a fix.

One of the air-conditioner vents was broken, and it rattled like a metal sign in the wind. Why was it so loud today? She glared at the ninety-seven-degree reading on her temperature gauge and snatched a pen from her front pocket.

This was so unlike her. Fear bubbled into irritation at the thought that she'd lost control so quickly. She smacked the pen on the AC vent. Impervious to her alpha personality, it kept rattling.

There was another thing, Chris realized. She'd just blown it with Sarah. Gone was the dating period, the getting to know each other and the excitement of the buildup. It had been an absentminded, irresponsible rush to sex.

But, oddly, it hadn't felt like sex. Her night with Sarah had seemed so natural and not simply some kind of score.

Chris drummed her pen against the vent even harder, and Abel whined from the backseat.

That's what made it so strange. Part of her slogged through

a mammoth-sized slurry of disappointment, and the other danced barefoot in the cool grass of a delightful memory.

Sarah's body had been amazingly responsive and so incredibly sexy that once they began kissing in the hallway, Chris had completely lost all sense of correctness and restraint.

The tennis match in her head, of happiness lobbing the ball over to guilt and then guilt returning it with an overhead slam, made it almost impossible to concentrate on her job.

Her radio crackled and a flurry of urgent orders came. Two fellow officers were fighting with a subject on Curson Street, north of Santa Monica Boulevard. They called for K9 backup. She threw her car in gear and flipped on her lights and siren.

Chris pulled up to the sidewalk, tires screeching as she unbuckled the seatbelt before her squad car came to a complete stop. Abel knew what the sound of the siren meant, and as soon as she'd switched it on, his excited bark rose in pitch, like he was frantic to jump into action.

Officer Cates and a rookie officer named Perkins were on the sidewalk fighting with a Caucasian man. He was at least six feet tall, about two hundred and fifty pounds, and not eager to surrender. The man was on the ground and the rookie was on top of his legs. Cates was on his chest, screaming at him to comply with their orders, but the man's flailing and ranting made it apparent that he was probably as high as a kite and wouldn't stop.

Chris opened the back door, grabbed Abel, and quickly latched a leash onto his vest. When she rounded the squad car and got to the sidewalk, she yelled, "Cates, back off!"

Cates and Perkins untangled themselves from the man, who was now shouting a string of half-intelligible curse words and still throwing punches at the officers. They were all on their feet and the officers pulled back, guns drawn.

"Stop fighting," Chris screamed. "Get your hands where I can see them!"

He refused and took a step toward her. As he did, Chris released Abel, who bolted like a rocket. In less than a second and a half, he launched upward and took hold of the man's upper arm. The man howled and spun around, but Abel held on like a vise grip cranked all the way up.

The man, now unconcerned with the officers, punched Abel in the head. Chris and her partners grabbed him and wrestled him to the ground. The man struggled, but Abel's well-planted teeth were taking a lot of the fight out of him. Abel continued to hold on while Chris and her partners wrestled his arms behind him and finally cuffed him.

She pulled Abel off, which was always a difficult task, given his drive and fixation. With the man now immobilized on his belly, Cates and Perkins stepped backward, both bending over to let their lungs calm down.

The man was now fairly lucid in his ranting. He wanted to kill the dog and kill all three officers. He demanded they remove the cuffs and reiterated his desire to kill them all.

Ignoring him, Chris raised her voice over Abel's barking and said, "Cates, you okay?"

"Yeah." He stood up straight, still panting hard, "Perkins, you okay?"

As Perkins straightened up, Chris saw a Cheshire-cat grin spread across his face.

"You didn't have to use the dog. I could have eventually gotten the asshole. I was ready to smash the guy in the face. It would have been fun."

"Fun?" Chris had heard that Perkins was a bit of a loose cannon, and that kind of comment was upsetting.

"I wanted to hear the crack of his cheekbones when I pummeled him. Instead, your dog got all the action."

Chris took a step toward Perkins. "That's what we're here for, so you don't get hurt and so you don't get written up for brutality, you turd."

"I can handle myself, Bergstrom."

Chris took another step toward him and Cates quickly moved between them.

"Thanks, Chris." He then mouthed to her, "I'll talk to him."

Abel had grown even more agitated at Perkins, who was obviously showing aggression toward Chris. His snarling turned into frenzied, salivating barks.

Cates told her he would handle the injured man and radioed dispatch, so Chris walked Abel down the street a ways to calm him down. She checked his body and head, running her hands over his neck, legs and chest, to make sure he hadn't sustained any injuries. When he didn't flinch, she took a deep breath in relief.

"Good boy," she said as she rubbed his coat, doubtful Cates could tone down the testosterone that circulated through Perkins's rookie head. Another wave of relief came over her. She hadn't faltered during the last confrontation, and the incident with the suspect had been serious enough to make her push thoughts of Sarah aside and focus.

Crap, she thought. Now Sarah was back again, invading her thoughts. Worse than those kitschy songs whose chorus would sometimes replay in her head, Sarah was a symphony orchestra belting out loudly.

"I'll follow you to Hollywood Community Hospital," Chris told Cates.

She had to stay with the suspect until the doctor treated his bites and she could photograph his injuries for her report. Unsurprisingly, they would have a long wait in the emergency room, and Chris settled in to the knowledge that visions of Sarah would continue to invade her thoughts and rattle her body.

❖

Monday afternoon came a little too quickly for Sarah. She'd slept in after Chris left and then lay in bed thinking about her for over an hour. If all the qualities Sarah had wanted were written down on a piece of paper, they would be on the personalized stationery of Chris Bergstrom.

Sarah hugged the pillow Chris had laid her head upon, remembering how amazing she'd been. She was beautiful and sexy and very funny. Her confident manner made her even more appealing. She was established in a great career and had a lot going for her. But more than that was the unexplainable chemistry between them that fizzed and effervesced. It had been immediate, drawing them together as effortlessly as a snowflake upon a child's nose.

Reluctantly, Sarah got out of bed and showered. She needed to hurry and dress if she was going to make it to lunch on time. Man, did she have something new to talk about.

She made it to Hamburger Mary's and found her friend Natalie sitting by one of the windows, away from the stage. That was a good thing, because the drag show was about to start and she wanted to be able to talk.

"Hey," Nat said as she sat down.

"Hey yourself. What's been goin' on with you?"

"I've been busy at the restaurant. Business is doing really well so I'm super busy with paperwork and ordering."

The waiter came over fairly quickly, which was also good because the place was filling up with people coming to watch the show, and the service would soon become slow. As soon as they ordered, a drag queen took the stage and announced, "Okay, you sloths, get your dollars out because this shit's starting."

A disco song came on and the MC started lip-synching to Donna Summers.

"What's up with you?" Natalie raised her voice over the noise.

"Same old, same old, except I met someone."

"You did? Who?"

"A cop named Chris."

"Were you speeding *again*?"

"Actually, I was shopping at Whole Foods."

"Have you gone out yet?"

"Last night. She came over for dinner."

"And she left after breakfast?"

"Not exactly. She left a little after midnight."

"How was it?"

Sarah couldn't help but smile. "It was really nice. She's funny and sexy and gets my jokes."

"She could be a keeper. Especially if she gets you out of tickets."

Their drinks arrived just as a drag queen, Sarah Jessica Parker's long-lost twin, took the stage. She must have been a favorite because the crowd began chanting, "Let your freak flag fly!"

"What the hell?" Sarah said.

"It's from *Sex in the City*. Haven't you watched it?"

"No. I'd rather read a good book."

"Speaking of books, how's the archeology course going?"

"Oh, I dropped that. It sounded great but I didn't like the class." She took a sip of her margarita. "I just can't find anything that holds my interest."

"You seemed to stay with the real-estate thing for a while. What happened there?"

"I could walk through houses all day long because I love the different styles and personalities, but my mom was pushing me so hard to hurry up and get licensed that I really started resenting the pressure. I'm thirty-five years old and she's still telling me what to do and how to do it."

"That sucks."

A shrill voice screamed into the microphone, "Damn, it's hot here in L.A. I just saw two trees fighting over a dog, so enjoy the air-conditioning, little darlings. And remember, we're not giving you all this glitz and glam and fabulousness for nothing. Give a bitch a dollar!"

The current drag queen was walking around the tables, bending over to allow patrons to shove bills into her cleavage.

"Now, that's not a bad gig," Nat said.

"If I had that much hair spray on my head," Sarah said, "I'd go up in flames at the nearest candle."

But she really admired those performers. They bucked convention and not only knew what they wanted, but were courageous enough to weather the conservative storm of right-wingers and gay bashers. Those drag queens were ballsy.

"So, are you going out with Chris again?"

"I sure hope so."

"I've known you a long time, Sarah, and I'm telling you this out of love. Just relax and enjoy her, okay?"

Sarah nodded, but her insecurities told her that was easier said than done.

❖

The calls had died down quite a bit. It was that weird space of time when even criminals got hungry and sought out a meal.

Chris was back at the station's parking lot, ready to go in and get some paperwork done. Abel was lying down in the back, not relaxing, because he was more than alert as long as he was working. He rested with his eyes open and let out an occasional breathy woof.

Chris flipped the cell phone over and over in her hand, contemplating a call to Sarah. Earlier that morning, her first inclination was not to call her. Ever. She'd made a rash decision and had no idea how to handle it.

What do you say to someone whom you've had sex with but barely know?

She knew what Paige would say. "Chill out, Chris. It's only sex."

But if sex was so simple and easy, what was precious and worth waiting for?

Still, she couldn't get Sarah off her mind. If they hadn't gone as far as they did, she would have called her hours ago to say hi and to ask her out on another date. But now, what was standard protocol?

More than once, Chris had picked her phone up only to drop it back on the car seat again. What if she never called her? Would Sarah eventually make the call? And what the hell would they talk about? The extremes were easy. A john would tell a hooker, "That was great, here's a little extra cash as a tip." And people in serious relationships would purr their affections and tell each other how much they loved each other.

Chris and Sarah's night together didn't apply to either. But nothing was as hot as the night they'd spent together. Even the wildfires raging around them couldn't generate that much heat.

Damn it, she really liked her. Was there any way to go backward? Was it possible to pretend the sex hadn't happened, progress to date number two, and behave in a more traditional manner?

Yeah, she thought. That was as easy as unelectrocuting a serial killer.

So now what? It had to be dealt with in one way or another. Should she wait until Sarah called and then act cool, like it was no big thing? Or should she call Sarah and explain the funnel cloud of turmoil that was spinning her up like Dorothy's pigtails?

Both sounded pathetic.

But maybe Sarah was feeling the same thing. They could talk about it and agree to reel it in a bit.

Chris tried to ignore the niggling realization at the back of her head that her body could now easily override her mind. Sarah's sensual mouth and arms and legs had driven Chris to nearly burst at the seams. And as much as she wished she could deny it, Sarah left her physically satisfied and unbelievably astonished.

The thoughts that spun around her began to fill the squad car, and she suddenly felt claustrophobic. She got out, leaving the car and air-conditioning running for Abel, locked it, and headed toward the station.

She got a few feet from the back door and looked down at her hand. Exasperated, she realized that a person with OCD wouldn't flick a light switch as nervously as she was flipping her phone.

"Shit," she said, and finally dialed.

"Hello?" Sarah's voice sounded wonderful.

"Hi, it's Chris."

"I figured that. I hear jail keys jingling in the background."

"You do?"

Sarah laughed. "I'm kidding."

"Oh." Now what? "How are you?"

"I'm great. I've been thinking about you. A lot."

If it were half as much thought power as Chris had expended, she'd still be drained. "Thinking what?"

"About us. Last night."

Please say that you had second thoughts about last night. "Yeah?"

"Uh-huh. Chris, I…we…us being together…"

Chris exhaled loudly. "I was thinking the same thing."

"It was incredible, wasn't it? It was so sexy and spontaneous. I really loved it."

She wasn't thinking the same thing. Oh shit. "Yeah…?"

"Are you being coy now? I wouldn't expect that from a Los Angeles police officer."

The station door opened, smacking into Chris. Cates poked his head around from the other side and mouthed, "Sorry."

"No, it's just that, ah…I'm brain-dead today."

"You'd be right about that," Cates said as he stepped out.

Chris punched him in the arm and he feigned a grimace before plopping his shoulder bag down on the sidewalk to rummage through it. Chris stepped away as Sarah said, "I'll apologize for that, but nothing else."

After an empty moment that Chris couldn't find words to fill, Sarah said, "Would you like to come see the wildlife refuge?"

"Yes," Chris said, knowing she shouldn't be relieved about the change in topic because the matter would continue to haunt her well through the night. "I'd like that."

"When are you off next?"

"Tomorrow, actually."

"Is it a date, then?"

Yeah, Chris thought, it could be a date, specifically date number two. The way a second date should be. She could handle being around Sarah without her pants heating up to a critical flashpoint. "Yes, it's a date."

Sarah sighed, and her sexy tone pierced Chris's ear and ricocheted through her gut and exploded between her legs.

As Sarah gave her the address, Chris wondered if a car thief in an auto museum would have a tougher time with willpower.

She'd barely hung up when Cates closed his bag and stood up. "A date? With who?"

"A women I met recently. She works up at the Angeles Crest Wildlife Refuge. I'm getting a tour."

"I've been there. Great place. My kids love the chimpanzees. I think it's because they're closer relatives to my little boogers than I think."

Chris opened the door. "You outta here?"

"Yeah. One chimp needs a ride to soccer practice and the other gets picked up at T-ball."

As the door swung closed she called out, "Don't forget the bananas."

❖

Chris typed out a request for Paige to call her, but it was usually never as simple or direct as asking her outright. Instead she did what she usually did and sent one of a hundred ditties she'd heard at the station.

A traffic cop pulled a man over for speeding. He walked up to the car and said, "I'll have to report you, sir. You were doing eighty-five miles an hour."

"Nonsense, officer," said the driver. "I've only been in the car for ten minutes."

She waited and then her phone rang. "What are you doin'?"

"Nothing much. Avalon's in New York meeting some producers." It sounded like Paige was killing an ant with a hammer.

"What the heck are you doing?"

"Fixing my printer."

Chris shook her head as she finished pulling on her jeans. "Why didn't you go with Avalon?"

"I've got a few appointments. Plus, she's only gone until tomorrow." The pounding continued. "Wanna go shopping? There are a couple of places in Santa Monica I'd like to check out."

"I'm going to the wildlife refuge center to meet Sarah. She volunteers there."

"So, a second date? Hey, you haven't told me about the first. Obviously, it went well."

It had and it hadn't. What she'd expected had been blasted out of the water by the shark that had erupted between her thighs. "It did. I mean, it was different, but yeah, it was good." The words came out slathered in hesitation.

The pounding stopped. "What was that?"

"What?"

"I know you didn't eat paint chips as a kid. What was the dithering about?"

"It was great, okay?" She put on her shirt and noticed it was on backward.

"Not okay. Now you're just blowing me off. What happened?"

As she fixed the shirt, she thought a moment. Gravity seemed to disappear when Sarah was close by. A light, lifting feeling overpowered everything else. As wonderful as it felt, it was a new experience and had unnerved her.

"She was wonderful. It's just that things went a little too far."

"You slept together."

"Yes," Chris said. "And I know what you're going to say. 'Relax, it's just sex.'"

"Well, obviously it wasn't just sex to you."

"That's what I mean! It's not something to casually engage in, like lawn bowling or whatever."

She heard Paige snicker.

"You know what I mean."

"I do. I only laughed because I suddenly had this picture of you on a bocce-ball court, naked as a jaybird. Listen, I know you're thinking you acted out of character. And I know you don't take sex lightly. But something must have made it okay to go that far. Or were you drunk?"

"No, I wasn't." Chris grabbed some shoes. "I don't know why, but we were in her hallway kissing and I got swept up in the moment."

"When did it become a bad thing?"

"When I woke up this morning."

"So last night was great?"

"Fantastic."

"The way I see it is, last night, your head took off and went on a drive or, in your case, a joyride. You were feeling, not thinking. And this morning, your head decided to come back and immediately started analyzing. Am I close?"

"Yes."

"Tell me one thing. Why wasn't your head present last night?"

Chris stopped tying her shoes. "I guess I didn't want to think. But that's the problem. I was careless. I don't even know her that well. This is starting out backward."

"Sex on the second date or seventeenth date has little to no bearing on the success or failure of the relationship. As long as you both were comfortable and wanted it, I think it'll be okay."

"Yeah, maybe."

"And don't underestimate what you said about not wanting to think too much last night. It felt good and you just went with it. Maybe you knew enough about her to trust that it'd be all right."

Chris took one last look in the mirror. Paige was right. Other than needing a haircut, she hadn't suffered any damage yet. "You're right."

"So go and have fun. And then call me and give me all the details."

"Okay."

"Did that help?"

"No."

"I thought so."

Chris knew her best friend was now smiling.

She got off the phone and went out to Abel's kennel. She let him out and he danced away, happily looking for his ball.

"Take a break," she said, and when he finished, she threw the ball for him a few times and locked him back up.

Trepidation still lurked inside her, hovering in the corners of her brain like unsettled little dust bunnies.

CHAPTER SIX

The drive to the Angeles Crest Wildlife Refuge was gorgeous. Other than the smoke-tinged skies, the scenery was tremendous. Wind blew the tops of the trees, and they bent over the shorter ones like parents checking on a child. She spotted a few birds, but not as many as she'd seen before. She hadn't been hiking in the area for a couple years and made a mental note to plan a trip soon.

Turning off the highway, she listened to the gravel road to the refuge crunch under her tires and smiled as she bounced along, happy to be going to see Sarah. On the way, she'd had the just-chill-and-don't-overthink conversation with herself about five times, so she was definitely ready.

Sarah walked out to meet her as she pulled into the visitors' parking lot.

"Hi," she said as Chris got out of her car.

They kissed briefly.

That went well, she thought, before telling herself that commentating was for sports reporters.

"Ready for the tour?"

"I am."

They walked down a cement path, past some buildings, and Chris could see large enclosures built into the hills to the right. Exotic noises came from every direction—screeching, howling, cawing—all sounding as if a political caucus was taking place.

"This entire facility is a rehab and medical refuge for native, wild, and exotic animals. We have a hundred forty acres here, housing and providing rescue, rehabilitation, and relocation to any animal that needs help. We get them from circuses, private parties, and animal exhibits. Some are injured in the wild, orphaned, or abandoned by their parents."

"You're very versed on all this. It sounds like you give a lot of tours."

"We all do."

"What kinds of animals do you have here now?"

"Let's see…lions, leopards, tigers, bobcats, primates, foxes, reptiles, bear, wolves, deer, and many birds."

"Wow."

"Close to forty thousand animals have been cared for over the years. We run twenty-four hours a day, seven days a week."

She led Chris to a row of large kennels on the lowest level of the hill.

"This is our wolf area," Sarah said, and stopped at the first kennel. "And this is Nala. She's been here for about two years."

Chris watched Nala walk toward them. She was stepping cautiously, her eyes never wavering from them. Though she looked a lot like a husky, she was much larger. Her thick, grizzled fur was ticked with brown and a little black, and Chris guessed she weighed anywhere from eighty to eighty-five pounds.

Nala reached the fence and sniffed the air.

"She came from Alaska," Sarah said as she knelt down. "She had serious facial trauma and a lot of battle scars. Her teeth were damaged," she pointed to a dark patch of fur on her shoulder, "and she had a gunshot wound."

"Poor baby," Chris said, frustrated that people could mistreat such beautiful creatures.

Sarah stood up. "She's a very high-strung, nervous little girl, but that's typical wolf behavior. She's doing so much better now."

They walked down the row of enclosures and Sarah pointed

out each wolf, some paired up and some who functioned better solo.

As they followed the path that rose up and around a small hill, Chris said, "Arizona, Utah, New Mexico—you've named a lot of states, just from where the wolves came from."

"These animals are brought here from all over the world. And each one has a personal story."

"So what kind of work do you do here?"

"A little bit of everything. The volunteers feed and work with the animals, repair fences, help in the office, construct habitats, run educational programs. Just cleaning the facilities involves hours of hosing down, and lots of scrubbing and steam cleaning."

"What's your favorite thing?"

"Really, everything. But some special moments are unforgettable." She stopped and turned to Chris, cupping her hands in front of her. "Last week, I was hand-feeding a baby bald eagle." Her expression, bright with fascination, captivated Chris completely.

"What do you feed a baby bald eagle?"

"Shredded meat."

"I guess that's better than a burger and fries."

Sarah took Chris's hand and it felt very natural. She liked the connection. Sarah led her to a large compound nestled in big-cone Douglas fir and some Ponderosa pine trees.

"This is one of our primate areas. These are Guinea baboons."

Chris watched as a group lumbered toward them. They seemed to be as curious as she was. When they reached the fence, one baboon pushed its way to the front.

"This is Sasha," Sarah said. "She's the boss. This is a troop of seven Guinea baboons. They're the smallest of the species and weigh between twenty-five and fifty-seven pounds. We think she's about thirty years old and we call her the furry old lady."

Chris nudged Sarah. "She just raised her eyebrows at us."

"They're great communicators. If they grin, they're saying 'I'm sorry,' and if they show those sharp teeth, it's 'Be careful or else.'"

Chris held up her hand, "Sasha, no offense, but I'd rather not see your pearly whites."

"These baboons break the tree rule. They live mostly on the ground." She pointed and said, "Their short fingers are better suited for ground foraging. And with their arms positioned under the shoulders, they can pick with one hand and balance with the other."

"What's Sasha's personal story?"

"She came from a man who had her in a shack off a highway in Arizona. It was a tourist trap and people paid money to stare at her. She'd been taken from her mother way too young, bought on the black market, and lived many years by herself. Someone emailed Angeles Crest, and she was rescued shortly after that."

"The guy let her go that easily?"

"He was in violation of some animal regulations. The asshole didn't have a choice." The furry old lady seemed to understand they were talking about her. She sat down next to the fence and leaned against it, pushing toward them.

"When she arrived here, we were afraid she wouldn't be able to interact with a tribe. But she blended in perfectly." Sarah nodded toward her. "It's amazing, because she never had a family—no one she could relate to or who cared about her. And now she's the matriarch."

"She's beautiful, too."

Sarah grinned. Chris could tell she was emotionally invested in Angeles Crest.

Sarah took her hand again and they walked a ways, past a large outdoor aviary that, Sarah explained, was home to more than a dozen species that, for the most part, had broken wing and beak injuries.

Rounding another small hill, they approached a pen that had to be three or four acres large. In it three big cats lived among sturdy, old-growth pine trees, medium-size wooden decks, three ten-by-ten-foot cement pens, and a grass-edged pond.

"This is our leopard pen," Sarah said. "The fencing is fourteen feet tall and welded with six-gauge wire. The owner picked this place because of the trees. Leopards spend more time lounging in trees than on the ground. They're exceptional climbers, so we had to find the most established trees because of that."

"What are the cement things for?"

"That's where they take a break while we go in there and clean the land and pond. It also provides shelter during a bad storm."

One leopard trotted up to the fence and Chris stepped back.

"You're safe as long as you don't stick a finger through the fence," Sarah said. "This is Mattie. She's about four years old. All three—that's Phinneas lying on the ground and Patty in the water—came from private owners who realized that a grown leopard isn't the same as a kitten. That's the problem with people who want to keep exotic animals. They have no idea what it takes and that it's usually a bad idea for them and the cat."

"They're so beautiful. I know it's wrong to think, but I just want to reach in there and pet their fur."

"I know what you mean. If you hang around long enough, you find that they're a lot like a domestic cat, except on speed."

Mattie hooked the fence with a claw and gave it a good shake.

Chris stared at the impressive show of strength. "And steroids."

"Every week, we feed over six thousand pounds of meat to our cats alone." She waved her arm toward the north, which must have been where other immense pens were located. "That includes the lions, tigers, and the rest."

Chris turned to face Sarah. The sun, covered in a smoky overlay, cast her skin in a deep glow, accentuating her tan. Volunteering here, with an obviously loving and caring heart, Sarah was just as beautiful on the inside as out.

"You love it here."

"I really do. It's not a real job, but—"

"It *is* a job. You might not get paid, but you contribute to an incredible cause. You should be very proud of that."

Chris noticed that Sarah's expression had shifted into what appeared to be sadness. It was possible that she was ashamed of not having a career, but Chris knew many people who got paid to do a lot less than Sarah. And a week-to-week paycheck wasn't more important than making a significant contribution to charity. Sarah began explaining the immigration process for the leopards, so Chris resisted delving further into the topic.

After another hour of walking around, Sarah took Chris back to the offices, where they had lunch in a small break room. She'd made a basket of deli sandwiches and fruit salad.

Sitting across from each other at a small table, Chris held up her sandwich. "This was nice."

"It's easy to work up an appetite hiking around all those trails. I didn't want you to get light-headed."

"The only time I get light-headed is when I stand up too fast."

"I'll have to remember that."

Chris laughed. "Speaking of remembering..." She poked a fork in her salad and brought up two speared blackberries. "Where have I seen these before?"

"Those," Sarah said casually, "are some of the ones you weren't speaking sweet nothings to."

"Oh, the neglected ones."

"That's right."

Chris leaned in close to the berries. "I love you just as much as the ones I took home. But I couldn't take you all. I hope you understand."

"Okay, you didn't tell me you were a weirdo."

"You didn't ask."

Sarah paused before saying, "Another thing I didn't ask was, how you are about last night?"

Chris stopped chewing. If her brain had been a mental CPU, rapidly processing the question to search the mainframe for a good answer, she quickly realized that the screen had just frozen. *Damn! What do I say?* And just as suddenly, she flashed on the four or five thousand times she'd stood in front of a suspect who had the same look she must now have. And she told herself what she always told them. *The truth would be good right about now.*

She put down her fork. "Last night was fantastic. Being with you was incredible."

Sarah studied her. Chris forged on. "There's just this thing. I mean, it's not a thing but a…thing. Okay, I'm not making any sense." She looked to Sarah and grinned nervously, hoping for indulgence. "I've never…I mean, that was the first time…"

"You've been with a woman," Sarah said. "Oh, shit, I didn't know."

Chris's flung her hands up. "No! That's not what I meant. This is the first time I've slept with someone so quickly."

Sarah looked down for the briefest of moments. "Oh, because of the incredible night we had, I was tempted to call bullshit on you."

"I guess it's been a rule of mine for a long time." Chris looked down at her sandwich as if the wrinkles in the lettuce would magically spell out better words to say. "I usually get to know someone pretty well before…" She looked up and couldn't read Sarah's face. She was screwing this up by declaring some stupid decree that now sounded just pathetically adolescent.

She reached out for Sarah's hand and was relieved when she felt it, strong and soft, in her own. "I just want you to know that, last night, I couldn't have given a shit about any rules. I went with what I was feeling, and even Sasha the baboon couldn't have pulled me away. Not that having Sasha there would have been good. That'd be kind of creepy, but—"

Sarah squeezed her hand. "I understand."

"You do?"

"Yes. And I imagine you were kicking yourself when you woke up this morning."

Chris grimaced from the truth. "I was. A little. So you know what I mean?"

"I know what you mean, but I don't feel the same way. I've learned that rules are the ugly concrete fences in an otherwise beautiful world. I suppose I'm at the opposite end of the spectrum in that I've been fucked up by following rules, so I usually ignore them."

"Maybe you shouldn't say that to a cop." Chris was relieved when Sarah laughed. "Sarah, it's not that I regret it. Well, I guess I regret not taking more time before last night. There's something to be said about a passionate buildup."

"There are lots of ways to achieve that."

"I guess there are."

Sarah released her hand and folded it over the other, resting them on the table and leaning closer to her. "So, what do you need right now?"

Chris hadn't thought that far ahead. She hadn't planned on anything but just getting the past days' worth of conundrums out. And now, seeing Sarah again and watching her as she talked about the animals, and appreciating how gracious she was being, Chris was as comforted as impassioned. "I know what I don't want," she said. "I don't want to stop seeing you."

Sarah plucked a blackberry from Chris's salad and offered it to her, and Chris opened her mouth. As Sarah slipped it in, her fingers lingered. An abrupt rush of adrenaline shot through Chris and detonated between her legs.

She waited until Sarah slipped her fingers out but still couldn't chew.

"Well, now we have two things in common."

A quick but pleasing shudder jump-started her mouth. "Uh, huh…?"

"I don't want to stop seeing you," she said, and then touched Chris's lip again. "And now you're a murderer, too."

Chris chewed on the succulent little berries. "I guess I am."

"So, where do we go from here?"

The tightness in Chris's pants told her to go straight back to Sarah's house. She clutched her fork as desperately as an overboard sailor grasps a life preserver. "I'm not sure."

While she knew her "rules" were more than likely archaic and naïve, she was still too afraid to keep speeding along.

Sarah then valiantly solved her Catch-22. "Let's just take it easy and see where it goes."

"Okay."

"I can't say that I don't want you, though."

"Believe me, I understand."

"And taking it easy shouldn't be difficult right now because I know I smell like a skunk that just mud-wrestled with a badger and a chimpanzee."

Sarah's compassion was beautiful, and it made Chris like her even more. "I guess now I have to admit to something else."

She paused until Sarah's expression grew serious.

"I have a thing for badgers."

Sarah walked her out to her car, and before she got in, Chris said, "Thanks for understanding. I know I must sound like an old maid."

Stepping closer, Sarah brushed Chris's hair back over her ear. "I was there last night, and that was no old maid in my bedroom."

Chris leaned forward and kissed her. It was gentle and sweet and spoke of good things ahead.

CHAPTER SEVEN

Fire officials are increasing staffing levels and getting resources in place by moving air tankers to bases across the state. In the meantime, seasonal firefighters will be brought into the Angeles National Forest starting this weekend."

Sarah watched TV while she waited for Natalie to pick her up. They planned to go to Melrose and shop, but she wasn't necessarily looking forward to it. Her gut felt tight and broiling again, and she knew what that meant.

"Fuck."

She turned up the TV, hoping she could forget the demons that had returned to visit. But the plight of the animals hit her hard. She understood the terror of a nightmare and the dire search for a way to escape.

"Fire crews in California have battled more than six hundred eighty wildfires, two hundred more than average for this time of year. Officials say the lack of rain is a big problem. The past winter was the fourth driest in Southern California in a hundred thirty-five years."

Her cell phone buzzed and she opened Nat's text.

I'm here.

Sarah turned off the TV and hoped to hell her mood wouldn't turn fouler.

❖

The sun always seemed to shine on Melrose Avenue. Sarah imagined that the businesses paid someone to guarantee it. There was certainly enough money changing hands and more influential power than a good day in Congress.

"You're in a mood again," Nat said as they wandered through Fred Segal.

Sarah frowned. She'd been quiet and voiced more than once that she didn't like anything in the store. But that's not what was bugging her.

"You know that woman I was telling you about? Chris?"

"Yeah."

"I saw her the day after our first date and she was kinda freaked out. She said she never has sex on the first date." She took a blouse off the rack, barely looked at it, and almost threw it back. "We talked about it, but I spent the morning thinking I've blown it with her."

"But you said you talked about it."

"We did." She shook her head, at the clothes and especially at the question. "She's so opposite from me, Nat. She's responsible and practical."

"You're doing it again."

Sarah scowled at her. "Fuck, Nat."

"Maybe you need that kind of person."

"It's never worked before."

"That's because you always undermine things."

Sarah's racing frustration was increasing in speed, and she knew the first target to crash into would be Nat. "Why am I shopping here?" She flipped the legs of a pair of pants that hung on another rack. "These things are four hundred dollars. Am I pretentious like this?"

"You're anything you want to be."

"What the fuck is that, Nat? Am I just a rich kid that needs to feel at home with my peeps?"

Nat began to laugh.

"I'm serious." She pushed Nat's shoulder.

"You can't keep being pissed at the world, Sarah. Do what the heck you want to do. Wear ripped jeans and a dirty T-shirt for all I care."

Sarah had held back when she talked to Chris the day before, and she was mad at herself for it. She wanted to tell her how much she liked her and how immediate the attraction was. Chris was the rare butterfly that lands on your hand and it's so beautiful that all you do is pray it never leaves. Chris represented the opportunity of a real relationship. Sure, their time together had been as brief as the blink of a firefly, but so much more magical. She was standing on the precipice of a chance that her gut knew could be so good and anxious because the edge she stood upon could quickly crumble underneath her in a heartbeat.

Under it all, though, she was scared she would soon awaken from what had to be a dream. "Let's get out of here."

As they walked down the north side of the street, they poked around in the clothing shops, and Sarah tried to urge her mind to just empty out all thought.

Nat dragged her into Vivienne Westwood to look for shoes, but Sarah wasn't that game. She wandered around, looking at the scads of clothing that hung gaunt and lifeless on their hangers, as if they were designed not for skinny models but for prisoners of war. Maybe that wasn't too far from the truth because most of the shoppers were barely a size zero. These clothes were perfect for them, not her.

She felt the buzz of a cell text.

Care to go out tonight? I get off work at 4.

Maybe she hadn't blown it with Chris. She answered.

The badgers aren't available, so it'd just be me.

I'm disappointed but I'll manage. How about dinner?

Sounds good. If you're interested, there's a party in Venice.

Great! Shall I pick you up?

Would love it.

20:00? Just kidding, 8:00?

Funny. And yes!

Sarah's stomach loosened up. She wanted Chris so badly and hoped to God the edge she stood on proved to be strong.

❖

The traffic on Santa Monica Boulevard was unusually light, which was as rare as a rainy day in Los Angeles. The calls had been steady, but nothing had devolved into arrests yet.

She turned onto Highland Avenue, whistling some lighthearted tune from a musical. She couldn't remember the name and most of the lyrics, but it was bright and cheery and had phrases like *swapping romantic gleams* and *carousing around town*. She hadn't been this energized in a long time. Sarah was everything she could have written on a what-do-I-want-in-a-woman list. She had a date with her later and enjoyed the little buzzes of anticipation that snuck up on her frequently.

Her world was new and promising, and she felt a frivolity that she thought had died when she'd gone through her last breakup.

Her phone vibrated and she wondered what Paige wanted.

Hey, I have a question for you. It was Sarah. *It's a little forward so you don't have to answer if you don't want to.*

Hit me.

Have you ever had sex in your squad car? Could you get fired for it? If you haven't, would you? Okay, that was 3 questions.

Chris felt a strange rush. She's never been texted something like this before.

1. I haven't. 2. Yeah, I could get fired for it, but that's not why I wouldn't do it. 3. There's no room to have sex in my car!

Are you kidding that you haven't? Would you think less of someone if they did?

Not at all.

Was this what Sarah was talking about when she said they'd take it easy and see where it went? Admittedly, the texts were rather exciting, and damn, if that familiar twinge wasn't creeping down her spine and toward her thighs. Her heart began to pound eagerly. Whatever they'd agreed to, Chris wanted to partake in this interaction.

I'm sure it's pretty close quarters in there.

Ah, yes, radios and stuff. Gotta be careful you don't accidentally hit the PA button.

So you ARE speaking from experience.

Just some fantasies, maybe.

Spill.

Chris hesitated. She was already worked up just from a few texts. She felt the dizzying exhilaration of an act that she knew was forbidden. She focused on her heart as it pounded hard and determinedly. And she'd never felt more alive.

Someone gets in my squad car and we start kissing passionately. Her hands are all over my uniform and she starts unbuckling, removing, unbuttoning, unzipping, unVelcroing...

You're giving me some great ideas...

I'm here to help. You're driving me nuts by the way. And she was. Chris had to adjust the way she sat, but no matter how she moved, lovely little twinges prodded her.

I think you're my hero.

I get to see you in two hours. Shall I pick you up?

Yes, please. I can't wait.

Oh, and did I answer your questions sufficiently?

It's a good start...It's a real good start.

Chris looked up from her phone, mesmerized. She was wet and she hadn't even seen Sarah, let alone touched her. She shook as another rush of desire rippled through her. This woman was like no one she'd ever encountered. The key, however, was to avoid getting run over by her own seemingly limitless new behavior.

❖

By eight thirty in the evening, the remaining tourists on the ocean boardwalk in Venice Beach had dwindled down to small numbers of people partying at the bars that dotted the promenade. The fortunetellers, artists, and buskers had packed up their gear and were somewhere else counting their tips. The surfers were long gone, and the only skateboarders were locals that were no longer carving it up at the skate park but now commuted from the liquor store to their apartments. Homeless enclaves, because it was safer to sleep in groups, wrapped themselves in blackened blankets and shared a nameless bottle of alcohol between them while they prepared their bed of sand or grass for the night.

The circus-like atmosphere was gone, but sticky remnants of ice cream and sodas marked the boardwalk, like they did every day of the year, the layers of grime chronicling the Southern California lifestyle of those who lived it and those who came to watch its spectacle.

Sarah and Chris strolled down the boardwalk, since it was the quickest route between one of the few parking spaces they could find and the party.

They hadn't talked much more about the sex thing, but Sarah felt a little bit of a change in Chris. Maybe she was tired, or possibly wary about being in Venice at night, but she also seemed the tiniest bit detached. Sarah also noticed that Chris's arm, now entwined with hers as they walked, felt slightly stiff.

"I haven't been down here in a long time," Chris said as they stepped over a broken pair of sunglasses and a dropped cup of some kind of blue liquid.

"It's been a few months for me. The party's on Wave Crest Court, on the next street up. My friend Patty lives there. She's a tattoo artist and has a party about every other month."

"When I think about the cleanup, that's a lot of parties."

Most of the streets terminated just behind the buildings on the east side of the boardwalk, so they crossed behind the Beach House Market and walked down a typically run-down alley, littered with whatever trash the ocean breezes had blown in, turning onto Wave Crest.

Even if Sarah had forgotten the address, it was obvious the party was going full tilt at the third house on the right. She could feel the ground rumble in time to the extremely loud hip-hop music, and the partiers who were in the front yard, yelling above the noise, sounded like a rowdier version of the New York Stock Exchange during a dump of expired stock options. This, of course, was pretty standard for a Patty party.

Sarah took Chris's hand and led her through the yard and into the house. It took her about ten minutes of maneuvering through the throng of people to find Patty, who was in the living room doing shots with three people that had more ink than clear areas on their skin.

Sarah hugged Patty and then introduced them. Patty grabbed Chris in a bear hug, which looked adorable, because of the crooked grin it produced from her date.

"It's about time you showed up again," Patty said to Sarah. And though she was already talking over the music, she said even louder, "Now who's ready for a shot?" She swung a bottle toward Chris. "Would you like one?"

"No," Chris said. "I'm good."

When Sarah waved the offer off, Patty said, "Well, if you're on DD duty, it's a good thing because not many of you are working tonight."

A gaggle of women appeared and immediately pulled Patty away.

Chris leaned toward Sarah. "Did we just get volunteered to drive people home?"

"No," Sarah said. "Nobody's gonna puke in your car."

"Of that, I am grateful."

Sarah looked around the room. She saw people she knew from previous nights at Patty's and some she knew from other parties. She didn't really hang out with many of them, but they were a hell of a lot of fun when the sun went down. This was a place to get crazy and dance and laugh and erase every care from your head. That's why she liked to come.

She hoped Chris would get the same out of it.

"If it's not a shot," she said to Chris, "what would you like?"

"On the way in, I saw a cooler in the kitchen."

"Okay, then." Sarah took her hand and they weaved through the crowd until they pushed their way over to the cooler that sat on the woodblock carving table on the other side of the kitchen.

Sarah opened it. "Nothing but bottles of Perrier in this one."

"That's perfect."

She scooped two out. "Okay."

Two hands grabbed her waist and she jumped. Behind her stood Felicia and Deb.

"What the hell?!" Sarah introduced them to Chris. "These two women are trouble. Don't talk to them."

Felicia threw an arm around Sarah. "We've learned from the best."

"Where've you been?" Deb said, eyeing Chris a little too conspicuously. "We haven't seen you for a while."

"I've been laying low, I guess."

"We were beginning to think you'd regretted your unforgettable performance."

Chris looked back and forth between them. "What happened?"

"Sarah, here," Felicia said, "was the star of the karaoke contest the last time she was here."

"You don't look the type," Chris said.

"Oh, she's the type—"

"Felicia…" Sarah squinted her eyes.

"Actually, she started the whole event."

"No, I didn't. Patty did."

"Patty got it going in the living room, but it was Sarah that moved it to the roof."

"The roof?" Chris looked at her, and Sarah couldn't tell if her expression of disbelief was good or bad.

Deb then said, "She had some guys lug up the sound system and gave quite a concert from up there."

Chris was still looking at her so she said, "What can I say? I like Abba."

"Abba?!"

Felicia laughed loudly. "Who doesn't like 'Waterloo' at about five hundred decibels?"

"She rocked it." Deb slapped Sarah on the arm. "But I think 'Fernando' was my all-time favorite."

"From the roof?" Chris repeated.

"Yeah! It was just like that video of the Beatles when they played on that rooftop and the police were climbing up to stop them."

"Yeah," Deb said, "except the L.A. cops don't wear those cute hats!"

"The police came?"

Sarah looked at Chris. "Yeah." It was a funny moment, actually. She'd been right in the middle of "Fernando."

Felicia pointed to Sarah. "One of the cops was trying to get her to stop, but she started signing like the song was about him!"

"And he loved it so much, he gave her a bracelet!" Deb was laughing in between each word. "Too bad it only lasted for the night."

"That was priceless," Felicia said, slapping Chris, who flinched.

Sarah hadn't thought of that night in a while. The look on the officer's face had been so deadpan, just recalling it made her laugh. She gave Deb a little push and turned to Chris. Suddenly, her stomach lurched.

The stunned look on Chris's face filled her with apprehension. Oh, this isn't good, she thought.

"Okay, ladies, enough rehashing. Chris and I are going to

get some fresh air." She didn't look at her but reached for her hand, leading her out to the front yard. The crowd of people had grown even larger, but she found a spot by the edge of the street and stopped.

"Chris, are you okay?"

"Were you arrested?"

"No, I was thrown into the police car. I saw the cop getting out his handcuffs, but he turned to react to someone running by him so I jumped out and ran."

Chris looked at the ground without saying anything.

"It was just a silly prank. At a party. That happens all the time."

"It happens all the time?" Chris's voice was calm, but she looked far from tranquil.

"It was a party, Chris." Little branches of guilt coiled around her gut.

Again, she didn't get a response right away. That familiar discomfort began to heat up inside.

"Okay, you know what?" Sarah tried to stem the fear that flowed quickly up her spine, but it was too strong. "Now *you're* getting that cop look, too."

At the same time Chris's chin dropped, her eyebrows rose. Though it wasn't about Chris exactly, Sarah had seen that look too many times before, and she tensed up to defend herself.

"It wasn't a big deal. Shit. It was fun, okay?"

"Hey, slow down." Chris reached for her but she pulled away.

I'm not safe, she began to chant silently. I'm not safe, I'm not safe.

"Sarah, I'm a cop," Chris said. "Of course I'm going to be surprised if someone I'm dating has been in trouble with the police."

"So, I'm a criminal."

"No! I didn't say that." She pointed toward the house. "If there were drugs in there, you know I'd have to leave, right?

Maybe I should have told you that before we came here, but I have to uphold certain ethics."

"And seeing me is unethical?"

"No, no. I was using that as an example of what makes my job different from a lot of others. I was just surprised that you had a tangle with the law. That kind of stuff gets my attention. I mean, if I'm dating someone who gets arrested, and I know you didn't, that isn't looked upon well in my world."

"Well, I *didn't* get arrested."

"I know. That's what I said." The intensity in Chris's voice decreased. "My life is orderly, Sarah. My world is about good and bad. I live within limits that make sense to me. When I was a kid, my parents ran the house military style. It was up at five thirty and off to school by six forty-five. They hammered the difference between right and wrong into me. That's what I'm used to."

While part of Sarah understood that Chris was trying to explain herself, the rest of her took each and every word as an attack. At the very least, it was a criticism. She wanted to lash out, to tell Chris no one was perfect, and that included cops.

Don't, she said to herself. Don't ruin this like you always do. Just say something without throwing all the kitchen knives along with it.

"Extremes are suffocating."

Chris paused as if her face had just been splashed with droplets of water. "Yeah, that's true, I suppose. But rules provide order. When things are black and white, it's so much less complicated."

"Maybe in your world. Maybe that made you the prize child in the family."

"I'm far from the prize child, Sarah."

"That makes two of us," Sarah said, her soft underbelly still exposed. "But I'm not stodgy, which is something my parents wanted me to be. I choose to be spontaneous and not worry about what people think."

"I'm not against being spontaneous. But you can find ways

to do it sensibly. Causing the police to come out to a party when they could be answering an important call isn't the highest measure of responsibility."

Sarah felt an armadillo-like shell forming around her. Yet again, she was a fuck-up. And the foulest part of it was that Chris wasn't all that far off the mark.

"Look," Chris said, "let's get out of here. Let's just go somewhere else and make this night great."

Sarah had no idea how to turn this around. "Yeah, well, I'm tired. I think I'd like you to take me home and call it a night."

She looked at the ground, unable to witness how Chris would react to her words. After a moment, Sarah heard her say, "Are you sure?"

She did the only thing she was good at. Lifting her head, she smiled as unaffectedly as she could, erasing any opportunity to continue the dialogue, and reached out for Chris. "Yeah, come on, it's late."

CHAPTER EIGHT

Thursday moved slowly for Chris. The calls came back to back until three that afternoon. She went back to the station to finish her paperwork and found Cates and a few others in the break room, watching television.

"What's up?" she said as she stepped in.

"All but one fire is out," Cates said as he jerked his head toward the TV.

A helicopter was broadcasting images of the Angeles Crest fire.

"...Los Angeles Fire Department called the fire aggressive, stating that it was moving quickly. Four more fire engines have been dispatched to the scene that's reported to be thirty percent contained. Five structures have been destroyed in this remote area since Tuesday. At a news conference yesterday, Governor Brown said that the state's budget crisis would not affect efforts to fight the fire and that the blaze presented a great challenge."

Moving quickly and a great challenge, Chris thought. That sounds exactly like Sarah and me. Still bothered by the night before, the conversation they'd had continued to skulk around the edges of her brain, the words curdling like a bad jug of milk.

Maybe she'd overreacted. People acted crazy all the time. It wasn't like Sarah got hauled in and booked. And the incident didn't reflect on Chris herself. Sure, she'd made it a point to stay away from bad apples. She'd abandoned a few friends because associating with them might harm her position on the force. Long gone were her days of hanging around even the fringes of drug users and stupid behavior. Admittedly, she'd gone to an extreme to keep those people well out of her life. It was important, especially when she'd just joined the police department, to notice trouble from a far distance and stay away. And it had been an easy lifestyle to maintain.

But Sarah didn't really fall into that category, did she?

Again, she didn't have many answers because she didn't know that much about her. It still amazed her that she'd allowed herself to fall in bed with Sarah so soon.

Blinking red lights meant stop. That was the most basic law of motor vehicles. Drivers move forward until they encounter a red blinking light. At that point, they stop to avoid a hazard.

Blinking red lights surrounded Sarah.

The news footage continued to cover the fires, and her fellow officers were talking about the firemen they knew who were probably out there in the midst of it.

Moving quickly and a great challenge, the reporter said. With red lights blinking.

It sounded like a collision course to her.

❖

Sasha sat as close to Sarah as she could. It was their special time, and Sasha had galloped over as soon as she saw Sarah walking up with a paper bag.

She was now enjoying a frozen pop, made with cherry juice and raisins, a treat the refuge would allow the Guinea baboons, especially during periods of unusual heat.

As Sasha turned the pop around and around, slurping and sucking her dessert, Sarah made conversation.

"I know you know what it's like to be so different from your own kind. You were away for so long, and when you returned, you were an outsider and no one could understand what you'd been through."

Sasha suddenly stopped slurping and lifted her head, stretching it toward the sky. Her nostrils flared and she sniffed rather loudly.

"It's the smoke," Sarah said. "It's all over L.A."

She pulled at some weeds that coiled their way around the base of a fence post.

"Chris must think I'm some kind of alien as well. Last night, she looked at me like I'd just murdered the pope. I mean, I'm not saying it was smart to cause the police to come to the party, but we were all just messing around."

With lips now starting to turn red, Sasha looked up at her curiously.

"That lipstick makes you look rather fetching, you furry old lady."

Deadpan, the baboon turned her focus back to the fruit pop.

"Chris has a point. I'm thirty-one, and I suppose I shouldn't be singing from a rooftop. At least not through a massive sound system."

Having finished her treat, Sasha chewed on the stick, looking cross-eyed as she stared at it. Sarah opened the bag and pulled out three large carrots with bushy green tops. Sasha immediately dropped the stick.

"Here you go," Sarah said, handing them through the fence.

As Sasha crunched away, Sarah continued to pull weeds.

"I guess it's not too much to ask that I don't cause that kind of ruckus anymore. But I don't want to turn into a prude. Life's meant to be enjoyed, isn't it? I mean, shit, if I wanted to be picture-perfect, I have two of the best role models around. But I'll rot in hell before I start acting like my parents."

She let out a sarcastic snort. "The fucked-up thing about it is my parents live a complete sham. At least Chris seems to live what she believes. God, I like her, Sasha," she said. "I just want to see her again."

Sasha fixated on the carrots, only looking up when Sarah crumpled up the bag. That got Tessa and Pudge's attention. They came loping up behind Sasha, but the older lady was ready. She turned around and let out a combination bark and screech. The two younger ones stopped immediately and sat down. They didn't seem interested in retreating but cautiously watched the furry old lady with envious curiosity.

A horn bellowed from the administration office and all four of them jumped.

"Oh, shit." Sarah jumped to her feet and took off running as fast as she could.

Madeleine was outside the main door when Sarah and about ten others rushed up. Allan stood next to her, reaching over to clasp her shoulder.

"We have to start evacuating. The fire is moving this way. We need to get the large animals out first. Sam and Rusty, get on the phone and call all the other volunteers. Willy, call the truck drivers from the list on my bulletin board. Their trucks are here in the parking lot, but ask if they can bring other drivers and use their personal cars and trucks to transport smaller animals. We'll take anything we can get."

The three men sprinted inside the office.

Adrenaline surged through Sarah. Though no one else was moving yet, images of running and chaos and animal shrieks clouded her vision. She saw the fire as a hurricane of flames engulfing the entire complex. Her heart pounded wildly as she pictured the frightened and distressed faces of hundreds of animals.

Please don't let it get bad, she prayed, please, please.

She heard her name.

"Yes, what?"

"Sarah, the cages are stacked together at the west end of the parking lot. Start pulling the cages apart and move the smaller ones to the enclosures. Then you and Allan begin loading them. You know which animals can go together in a cage. Keep them there, and when the large animals are loaded, we can move the smaller ones down to the lot."

The sound of Allan slapping her arm was like a starter's gun, propelling them in a dead run toward the parking lot.

"Oh, shit, let's start with the deer and her twin fawns," Allan said as they ran.

Sarah tried to respond but terror jammed her throat.

❖

Chris turned to leave the break room when one word of the reporters' commentary punched her in the ears.

"...refuge..."

She spun around and listened as the camera was now showing the studio announcers, who clutched papers at their desk, earnestly leaning forward.

"...the evacuation call came shortly after three thirty p.m. Let's try to get a report on exactly how close the fire is to Angeles Crest Animal Refuge..."

Cates turned to Chris. "Isn't that where your girlfriend works?"

Before she could answer, all their radios announced, "L.A. Fire needs multiple units, code three, for emergency evacuation at Angeles Crest Animal Refuge..."

She grabbed her microphone and held the button down. "Frank K-9 en route."

Cates got up from his chair and keyed his button. "Three Lincoln Seven Seven en route."

Chris was already down the hall, Cates right behind her, when, grateful, she heard the fall of dominoes as each of the other officers responded similarly.

❖

Sarah squinted as the acidic, sickly sweet wood smoke burned her eyes. The increasing heat had her soaked in sweat, which also ran into her eyes, but she couldn't slow down. Allan rolled a crate containing a wolf toward the parking lot as Sarah maneuvered another crated wolf right behind him. Ash flakes fluttered to the ground like a hideous gray snowstorm. She kept glancing toward the hills and was relieved when she didn't see any flames, but the intensifying wind foretold an ominous fact. The wildfire was getting way too fucking close, way too fast.

They reached the parking lot where a fire engine was unloading hoses. Two engines had already made their way down the frontage road to the north end of the complex to set up a perimeter.

Other volunteers helped Sarah and Allan load the wolves into two large vans. Many trucks had already left more than twice, heading toward local zoos, fairgrounds, and stables. Some had returned and were being loaded again.

Sarah guessed that at least eighty people had arrived, helping in whatever way they could. Some people came out of the vet quarters, carrying towel-wrapped animals and birds, while others led more docile creatures by lead ropes. Most of the large animals were already gone, but they still had numerous others to evacuate. Thankfully, most were the smallest animals in cages, ready to carry to vehicles.

Madeleine, bullhorn to her mouth, barked orders that were immediately followed as people peeled off in various directions. The organized pandemonium worked remarkably well, but they were still dangerously behind. A guy named Pete, who had just started volunteering a week ago, followed Madeleine around, calling out fire updates as he scrutinized his iPhone.

Sarah and Allan ran up to Madeleine and waited while she gave orders to four others.

"You two round up the last of the foxes," Madeline said, holding her hat down on her head as the winds started picking up. "They have to go one in a cage. And when you're done, get on the phone. We need more help!" She turned to another pair. "Are the chimps gone?"

One of them nodded.

"Then help Shelley and Connie in the reptile building. The snakes can go in burlap sacks if you don't have enough terrariums."

Dutifully, they ran off into the now-russet haze of the gusty parking lot. Madeleine took her hat off and stuffed it into her pocket. She turned toward Sarah and Allan with a look so stressed and tired, Sarah thought she might collapse.

"We really need help," she said to the both of them.

"Are Sasha and the rest out?"

"No, not yet. We've run out of cages."

Panic rose in her chest. "Madeline, what can we do for them?" Her bond with the furry old lady was stronger than any animal or person there. Anyone in her life, actually.

"Maybe we can call…" Madeleine stopped suddenly and cocked her head toward the refuge entrance. Sarah heard it at the same time. Sirens howled, and soon red and blue lights cut through the smoke as eight squad cars screamed into the parking lot.

"Chris," Sarah said out loud, and ran toward them.

Chris jumped out of her car and caught Sarah in her arms. "Are you okay? What do you need?"

Before Sarah could answer, Madeleine was right behind her. "We need transport help. But we're out of cages for the baboons."

Chris jerked her thumb backward. "All these squad cars have caged backseats."

"They could shit, you know."

"So do the criminals."

Madeline paused long enough to say, "Sarah, Allan, you two handle this, please. Thank you, all of you," and she sprinted away, hollering into her bullhorn.

Chris turned to wave her buddies over, and Sarah reached for her other arm. "Thank you."

"No worries. We're here to help."

Sarah kissed her quickly and said to the officers, "Follow us."

In minutes, all the cars were lined up at the baboon enclosure. A seasoned refuge handler had each car pull all the way up to the gate, and one by one, he caught the baboons and quickly led each of them to a car. Bananas helped distract them, and within twenty minutes, all but Sasha, who had avoided the roundup, were ready for transport.

Chris moved Abel to the front seat and pulled her car up to the gate. Sasha avoided the handler, screeching when he got close. After a few tries, Sarah called out to Chris.

"Do you have a bag in your car?"

Chris jumped out and opened the trunk. Moving equipment aside, she pulled out a paper bag, emptied it of dog treats, and ran it over to her.

Sarah pressed her face into the fence, rumpled the bag loudly, and called out.

"Sasha, Sasha, here." She waved the bag, hitting it with a banana to make more noise.

Sasha hesitated, looking between Sarah and the handler who was moving up behind her.

"Sasha," she called again.

Making her choice, Sasha trotted over to the fence and, when she got close, Sarah threw the bag into the backseat.

Sasha climbed in to grab the bag and tried to jump out, but the trainer was right behind her, quickly closing the door.

"That's all of them," he said.

"Let's get back to the parking lot. Madeleine will tell you where to take them."

"Los Olivos Farm has room for the baboons," Madeleine told the officers. "They're in North Hollywood, off Tujunga on the 118 freeway. They're waiting for you."

"I know where it is," Chris said.

"You're all angels," Madeleine told them, holding her hand to her heart.

Cates nodded. "This will, by far, be the most interesting ride of the day."

Perkins, the rookie that Chris and Abel had assisted when Cates called in the fight with the huge man, said, "At least we won't have to search these guys."

The officers got in their cars and Sarah walked Chris to hers.

Abel barked constantly, not understanding why someone else was in his kennel. Sasha shrieked back, but they both seemed more interested in badgering each other than in fighting.

Chris got in her car. "That's going to give me a headache,"

"You have no idea how much this means to me," Sarah said, bending toward the window. "And I'm sorry about the other night."

"Me, too. Hey, let's just get everyone safe and we can talk later, okay?"

Sarah nodded, allowing the relief she felt in the moment to cut through the tension that had all but consumed her.

"You gotta get out of here, too, Sarah."

"I will. We're not done yet, and I have to stay until all the animals are out."

"I know you do." Chris reached up and touched her cheek.

Sarah leaned in and they kissed.

"Be safe," Chris said. "I'll come back as soon as I drop Sasha off."

Sarah stepped back and Chris got on the radio. "Code three, fellow baboon warriors."

With lights and sirens blazing and blaring, the caravan of squad cars left, and Sarah felt a moving current of desire wash through her like the vortex of a whirlpool, sucking her down to a place she would willingly go.

❖

It was dark by the time Chris returned to the refuge. Three fire engines were in the parking lot, and the firefighters were resting on and around the trucks. That was a good sign, Chris thought.

She pulled up next to them and Abel began barking. Telling him to quiet down, she got out of her car.

"What's the status?" she asked one of the firemen.

"Seventy percent contained. Moved to the east, away from here."

"How close did it get?"

"Singed the back of the refuge. About four hundred feet of a fence is gone and some trees, but that's all."

"Thank God," Chris said. "And thank you."

He nodded and Chris went to find Sarah.

Many volunteers were still there, but now, instead of running, they were walking. Another good sign. They still had electricity, too. Chris stepped into the office and was greeted by a group of dirty and exhausted volunteers and a welcome cup of coffee.

They thanked her but she quickly waved them off. "You're the real heroes. You all were amazing today."

Sarah walked through the door and Chris's heart jumped. She looked completely drained, and soot blotched her face. Her clothes were filthy, and she had bloody scratches on her arms.

Chris reached for her. "What happened?"

"A baby raccoon wasn't too happy about leaving her warm cage in the vet clinic."

"You need to get that looked at."

"I will. Allan got it worse from a savanna lizard." She gestured toward a row of cabinets.

Allan was leaning against them and turned when he heard his name. Chris saw he had a six-by-six-inch bandage on his forearm. He held it up, as he would a cocktail. "I'm just glad I got the front end, not the business end."

"The savanna is a monitor lizard, and their best defense is a whipping tail that can cause serious damage. Allan was watching the tail when he was bitten, but he pulled away before the lizard got the whole mouth around his arm."

Chris cringed. "Ouch."

"It's not so bad," Allan said.

Sarah introduced Chris to Allan and the rest. Though worn out, everyone chatted animatedly, laughing and hugging a lot. The door opened and Madeleine walked in.

An eruption of cheers filled the room, and Madeleine put her hands up to quiet them.

"We did it," Madeline said. "All the animals are safe, and they wouldn't be without each and every one of you. We work every day to protect them from the evils of mankind, but sometimes, we have to protect them from nature as well.

"Today was a long day, and, other than some fences to repair, it looks like the refuge made it through intact."

Volunteers clapped and some whistled in delight.

"I hope you'll all be available to help bring them back when the fire department, those lovely angels, gives us the all-clear."

Sarah leaned toward Chris, "Looks like the black-and-white baboon taxi will soon be back in service."

Chris chuckled. "That actually works out because I think Sasha left her coat in my car."

After Madeleine finished, the volunteers began to leave.

"Let me walk you to your car," Sarah said. "I'll get my keys and leave with you."

The parking lot was emptying out, everyone driving around the fire trucks that were staying well into the night.

Sarah unlocked her door and turned to face Chris.

"You were right about the karaoke thing. It was stupid, and I don't blame you for being surprised about it."

"I've been thinking about it, too, and I tend to overreact. Sometimes I'm about as flexible as a corpse with rigor mortis."

"Well, you're a cute corpse."

"I have trouble just having fun sometimes. My life is black and white, I admit. And what I like about you is that you seem to just live in the grays, without worrying about things."

"Maybe we can strike a balance." Sarah put her arms around Chris. "Let's meet in the middle. We could try to have fun without breaking the law."

A fifty-pound lead collar had just been lifted off her. "Deal."

"And as far as I know, Officer, kissing in public is not against the law."

"No," Chris said as they moved even closer, "it isn't."

❖

With the Angeles Crest fire now contained, the city was in what officials referred to as a holding period—that time during fire season when nothing was blazing, but it was just a matter of time and one careless cigarette.

Sarah was at the refuge for the return of the animals, and they were now almost back to normal. A fencing company had volunteered to repair the burnt sections on the north end of the compound. A construction company offered to clear a firebreak around the entire refuge, and the rumble of bulldozers in the distance had been filling the air all morning.

Nat was with Sarah, sweeping up a massive amount of dirt, debris, and ashes. The pathway by the area in the emptied lion area that the firemen had set up was now full of trailed-in muck and branches.

"Thanks for coming out to help," Sarah said as they started sweeping, back to back, and moved away from each other.

"I'm so sorry I was with my aunt that night you evacuated."

"She was in the hospital. I wouldn't have expected you to leave her."

"It was just gallstone surgery. It wasn't like she was dying or anything."

"Still, you needed to be with her. She has no kids and no other nieces or nephews."

"I'd have rather held a baby chimpanzee's hand than my cigarette-breath aunt's."

"A chimp's breath isn't any better."

Nat stopped sweeping and held up her hand, pinching her fingers together. "Yeah, but their little oochy, oochy faces are so darn cute."

Sarah laughed. They were pretty adorable.

"How's the cop?"

"Chris? Great. She invited me to her K-9 trials."

"What's that?"

"A competition between K-9 officers all over the state. They perform tasks as if they were on duty, and the public is invited."

"So you get to watch Chris get all butch and stuff?"

Sarah laughed, although the thought had most definitely taken over a lot of her brain capacity since being asked. "Kinda."

"And everything's okay between you two? I mean, you called me and said you blew it because you took her to Patty's party in Venice."

"We talked it out. We're going to try to meet in the middle. I'm going to chill out a little and she's going to loosen up."

"Do you have to change? I mean, isn't that a bad thing to do—change for someone else?"

"I could definitely use some adjustments in my life, Nat."

"As long as you do it for you."

Sarah was nearing the end of the pathway, sweeping ashes that swirled around her feet. She listened to the *shoosh-shoosh* cadence of her broom as she considered Nat's advice. She should have started making better choices a long time ago. But she wasn't worried about making changes. She needed to confront the compulsion that pushed her to do what she'd always done.

"What do you want me to do with this?"

Sarah turned to Natalie, who was holding up something that looked like a dark pancake.

"That's lion shit."

Nat screamed and threw it over the fence. It sailed like a Frisbee and struck a tree.

"That was gross."

"I'd recommend avoiding anything that looks like a cow patty."

"Thanks for telling me now." Natalie brushed her hands on her pants. "Speaking of cows, you remember that nasty neighbor of mine? The one that hated everyone and would leave nasty notes about how we all parked or where we placed our trash cans?"

"What I really hated was that she'd throw rocks at dogs and spray little birds with her hose to keep them out of her trees."

"We had to have rounded up at least fifty real-estate for-sale signs to put on her front lawn."

"The one we handmade was the best." Sarah waved her hand through the air. "For sale, three-bedroom home. Husband left me for a twenty-two-year-old. Burn marks in carpet from torching his clothes. Gem of a house except for asbestos and natural-gas leaks. Rocks and spray hose not included."

"And I think she stopped bothering the birds and dogs after that."

"That was priceless."

"So you're going to stop having fun and being silly like that?"

"No," Sarah said, feeling the weight of what she needed to do. "It's the darker stuff."

Natalie stopped sweeping and looked at her in the way she had many times before.

Sarah chewed her lip. "Do you know what I mean?"

"Yeah, honey, I do."

❖

The K9 trials were held in Manhattan Beach on the high school football field, and Sarah found parking close to the event. Chris had invited her to come watch the Sunday portion of competition.

The field was set up with all sorts of obstacles for what looked like climbing and jumping. A few cars were parked in the middle, and smaller areas were fenced off with an orange plastic-barrier material.

An officer with his dog on the field stood waiting on one end, with three men, probably judges, on the other end, holding clipboards. As she climbed up and took a seat in the grandstand, an announcer was talking.

"Officer Flores, from the Pico Rivera team, and his dog Rado are on the field now. As we mentioned before, they will compete in various field exercises, and most will be timed. Because the building, narcotics, and explosives searches must take place in a controlled environment, we conducted that part of the competition yesterday. However, mock demonstrations will be performed during some of the intermissions. Please visit our vendors, who are on the track. We have safety and crime-prevention booths, raffles, child fingerprinting, and canine- and police-related products for sale. We also have canine, SWAT, and fire vehicles on display, as well as a police helicopter."

Groups of officers and their dogs were scattered all along the track that ran around the football field. She searched the groups, looking for Chris, and found her close at the other end of the grandstand. Like everyone in her group, she held the leash of a beautiful dog that seemed to pay total attention to her.

As the first competitor ran through a scenario, Sarah climbed down a few rows and across toward Chris, who turned as she approached. Her immediate smile widened, and Sarah had to admit she was just as cute as she'd been the day they met in the grocery store.

Chris broke from her fellow officers and came over to the stands.

"Hey!" she said, and kissed her.

"So, this is Abel," Sarah said, not sure if she should touch him. With his short-cropped mahogany and tan fur and the black mask and ears that were super alert, Abel was much more gorgeous up close.

"It is," Chris said, giving him a command to sit.

"What language is that?"

"It's Dutch. He was born and trained in Holland. By speaking Dutch I don't have many bad guys replicating commands like *stop biting*."

"Will he bite me if I get near him?"

"Not generally. If you tried to hit me or made an aggressive move, he might, to protect me, but he's trained to listen to my orders." She said something else to him, and he got up and moved to Chris's left side. "Say hello to him."

Sarah reached down and patted his head. He smelled her quickly and gave her hand a lick.

"He's pretty hyped up because he knows he's going to work today."

"When are you competing?"

"We're up after the Pico Rivera team. The first event is handler protection. I go up to a suspect and get attacked. Abel then goes after the bad guy. We'll also run an agility and obstacle course later." She took Sarah's hand. "I'm really glad you could make it."

"I've never seen K9s work. Plus it'll give me a glimpse of your world."

The announcer began and Sarah took a seat. Watching Chris from a distance allowed her to stare in a way she couldn't close up. The tight line of her uniform and the pronounced muscles in her forearms were sexy as hell. She admired Chris's concentration, even when she was on the sidelines of the event. Sarah felt proud to be there with her. Chris had accomplished so much in her life, and it delighted her that they were dating. Chris looked over at her a few times and she waved. All of the officers looked so put together and in command, but Chris stood out. It wasn't because she was the only woman there, but because she was the only woman for her.

The handler-protection competition was both remarkable and surprising. She watched as each dog received a command to lie down, at the ready, as his or her handler went over to a man in a bulky bite suit. The two men would yell at each other, and the dog would stay until the guy in the suit raised his hand to the handler. Like an explosion, the dog would launch itself toward the bad guy and bite him. Some dogs would start after him too soon, but each one would literally fly through the air to latch onto the guy's upper arm.

It was especially exciting when the announcer said, "Officer Chris Bergstrom, from the Los Angeles Police Department, and her dog Abel. Chris is one of only two female K9 officers in the LAPD."

Sarah watched Chris and Abel go through the exercise, feeling a now-familiar twinge of desire. Abel's bond with Chris was obviously strong. His muscles twitched before he sprang, and as soon as the man in the bite suit raised a hand to Chris, Abel took off at a full run. Leaping into the air, he bared his teeth and they flashed, and he was on the suited man, spinning him around until they both fell to the ground, Abel's teeth still embedded in his arm. Chris pulled Abel off the man, and as the audience clapped, she patted his side and scuffed up the fur on his head. Chris looked so together and irresistibly tantalizing. In that moment, Sarah felt the excitement of an enthusiastic fan watching a sexy superstar onstage.

She mentally stripped Chris's clothes off, wishing she were between her legs and taking as much command as Chris was right then. She wanted her. She actually needed her. The dim ache that inhabited her entire body ever since they'd been together now flared into a serious blaze. And unlike the blaze at the wildlife refuge, this was one inferno the fire department couldn't put out.

Only one woman, the gorgeous and wonderful one who was

now receiving applause from the grandstand, could come to the rescue.

Sarah watched Chris walk Abel to a group of officers on the sidelines. They talked amongst themselves, probably giving Chris their observations of her performance. The announcer called the next officer, and a guy in her group took his dog out to the field.

Sarah pulled her phone out and typed.

I know we're supposed to cool it a little, so is it inappropriate to tell you I think you're hot?

She hit the send button and waited. After a moment, Chris reached for her phone. She paused and then searched the grandstands, smiling widely when she found her. Then she looked back down at her phone.

Sarah's phone buzzed.

Hell, no! You just made my day! Well, and you coming here to the K9 trials.

You were great. I loved watching you and Abel.

There's going to be a break after this so they can set up for the agility course. Care to go for a cup of coffee or something?

Sarah looked up from her text to see Chris watching her. She nodded yes.

❖

Chris and Abel approached Sarah in the parking lot. They looked so regal together.

Chris told him to sit, and Sarah patted his head. He wagged his tail ferociously and seemed rather pleased.

"Stand right there," Chris said, and backed Abel up about

four feet. She called another command, and Abel charged over to Sarah's left side and sat. As he did, he pushed into her and she laughed.

"Wow!"

Chris pointed to her feet and Abel went back just as quickly.

"Canines are the most loyal partners an officer could have. And it's a plus that they don't chatter or disagree."

"Sounds like a perfect work environment."

"Other than being covered in dog hair within the first five minutes of my shift, driving a car that smells like a wet dog in the winter, and often having dried dog slobber on my uniform, yeah, it's the best." Chris held her hand out, inviting her to the car.

Chris put Abel in the back of her squad car and joined Sarah in the front seat.

"This is my first time in a squad car," Sarah said. "Well, the front seat, I mean."

Chris chuckled, happy that they'd talked about their minor clash at the party. She pulled out of the parking lot. "Sometimes we need to keep a closer eye on our suspects."

"And what if I'm really bad?"

"You get to go back there and sit with Abel."

Sarah turned around and saw Abel's nose pressed up against the screen. He took a few sniffs and woofed.

"That's a good incentive to fly right."

"He's the best."

"So he can find a person by sniffing them out?"

Chris nodded. "His olfactory locating system is tremendously more advanced than ours. We all have these odor-detecting patches high up in the nasal passages. Humans have about five or six million cells in these patches. Dogs have two hundred twenty million."

"I hope I wore deodorant."

"I think that's why he barked at you."

Sarah punched her leg.

"We use the dog's abilities, but they can't reason. We have to be the thinking part of the K9 team," Chris said. "For instance, I was on routine patrol one night. Another officer reported that a vehicle came back stolen and they were in pursuit. About five miles later, the subjects stopped and bailed out. The officer lost the driver so he called me while they set up a perimeter. I let Abel start where the stolen car was. Dogs have a scent cone that they follow until they find the area that's strongest, and when they hit on it, they lead us to where they need to go. So Abel was charging through a field and then some brush. I had him on a long lead and he was just tearing it up.

"The driver thought he could ditch us by hiding inside this big, old BBQ outside of a Southern Steak and Ale restaurant. Abel hit on it and was able to decipher the suspect's smell among the ash, charcoal, and dried meat and sauce. When I opened the top, he was hiding in the fetal position and started screaming, 'Don't let that dog get me, I give up!'"

"I can't say I blame him. I watched Abel fly through the air and bite that guy in the suit."

Chris pulled into a drive-through coffee shop.

"Do you mind if we get drinks to go? I have to be back at the competition soon."

"Not at all."

As they ordered, Sarah placed her hand in Chris's. It was so soft and warm Chris wanted to close her eyes and focus all her attention on just that one sensation. It brought back the night at Sarah's house and the feel of that same hand massaging, tickling, and playing lightly across her entire body. Chris pulled her in and their lips and tongues met, eager and consuming. The sound of her amplified breathing made Chris dizzy. She moaned, and Sarah bit her lip provocatively, tugging with what felt like urgent longing.

Sarah's hand was now gripping Chris's thigh with the strength of a cowboy grasping the reins of a bull. It was fervent and crazy and sexy. Chris might as well have dropped a lit torch in her crotch because her hips moved involuntarily. Helpless, she groaned at the extreme desire that abruptly seized her, and Sarah just gripped harder.

The drive-through window opened, and, reluctantly, they pulled away from each other. Chris's flushed cheeks burned from the sudden eruption between them, and she avoided eye contact with the barista.

Chris took their drinks, trying to calm the shaking as she handed Sarah hers.

"Oh, my God," Sarah said quietly.

Chris looked directly into her eyes, seeing an intoxicating intensity that had been there a few minutes before. "I love the way you kiss."

"Really?"

"I can't say that I've kissed a whole lot of girls," she said as she pulled out of the driveway, "but of all of them, you really are the best. You are so…so present. You're right there with me. Does that sound stupid?"

"Not at all. I understand completely. And it means a lot to me."

Chris took a sip of her iced coffee, giddy that Sarah was here with her.

"You got me a little worked up," Sarah said.

"Yeah, well, try wearing a wool uniform."

For the next block, Sarah swirled her cup of iced cappuccino.

I could fall so hard for her, Chris thought. What harm could come from just simply letting go? Sarah would catch her, wouldn't she?

Chris hadn't expected to meet anyone, but Sarah had come into her life, and suddenly those things that would normally fill her mind—training and work—seemed to get quickly diverted to a backseat.

Now, all she could think of was making Sarah laugh and just being close to her. She thought about holding her and the sounds she made in bed. A desire to learn more about Sarah and treasure every detail permeated Chris's brain. She wanted to know what she liked for dessert and how many hours she needed to sleep at night. Why had she gone to the store that day? What was her favorite movie?

She wanted a crash course but longed to slowly become saturated with the essence of her.

She turned her eyes from the road and watched Sarah as she looked out the window. Her fingers clutched her cup, and again Chris envisioned them tickling her skin, focused solely on her and driving her mad.

After taking a sip, Sarah said, "It's really great to see you and Abel work. It must take a lot of training."

"It does. Abel and I are together for ten hours a day on our shift, but I also work with him during my off time. We have these competitions, and we also do demonstrations at city and county functions."

"You said before that you prefer Abel to a human partner."

"Other than the fact that he's a horrible conversationalist, yes. I see my other partners when we back each other up on calls. But I don't have to deal with a personality that I don't want to sit in the car with all day. And while I trust all my partners, and they trust me, their loyalty can't match what Abel shows me. I rely on him, and I have all the faith that, if it ever came to that, he'd save my life."

"Wow."

Judging by the way Sarah turned to gaze out the window, it seemed there was more behind her response.

"Does that surprise you?"

"No. Dogs are remarkable." She continued to look away. "You live in a world full of people you can trust. I'm not sure I've ever felt anything like that. In order to have trust, you have to have faith. It means being able to predict what other people will do and believe that the outcome is what you think it'll be. I guess, in a way, the people in my life are pretty predictable, so I can depend on them acting a certain way. But it usually isn't in the way I need. If you see a behavior often enough, then the law of probability gives you a high confidence level that you'll get what you need. But do I have the kind of faith that allows me to be vulnerable?" She shook her head. "No."

"What about your family? Don't you have people you rely on?"

Sarah turned back to face the road. "Yeah. I can rely on the fact that my parents are going to get shitfaced tonight. I know my siblings will be critical of me. But would they protect me or let me be vulnerable? Not my family. It's a long, dreary story." She sipped her drink. "I suppose I trust Nat, my best friend."

"That's a good thing."

"It is." She looked at Chris. "And I trust that if I were to jump out of this car, strip, and run around naked, you'd arrest me."

"Maybe after taking a few minutes to observe the crime in action. But you're talking again about the law of probability. It's no different than putting money in a soda machine and expecting a can to drop out. I suppose having confidence that Abel will protect me can be seen in the same light. After all, he's trained to get between me and someone who poses a threat, but even without training, dogs can inherently protect you because they've allowed themselves to be vulnerable with you. You take care of them and they develop trust. In turn, they protect you."

They got back to the competition and parked among the rest of the squad cars.

"Yeah," Sarah said, "I get that. But sometimes you learn that you can't be vulnerable with people."

They heard a whistle, and Chris turned to see one of her K9 buddies frantically waving to her.

"I guess I'm up next."

They got out of the car, and Chris hooked Abel's leash up and got him out, too.

"I need to go," Sarah said when they met at the front of the car. "I'm late for something. Do you mind?"

Sarah's mood had definitely changed. The difference was slight, like the shift of a shadow over time. "No, of course not. I'm really glad you came out."

They hugged and Chris kissed her.

She watched Sarah walk to her car, and the urge to call out to her suddenly pulled at her.

"You're up, Bergstrom!" Her buddy whistled again. "Come on!"

"Shit." Chris gave Abel the command to go and blew out a breath of frustration, unable to talk to Sarah about what was bothering her.

CHAPTER NINE

Only advertisements and offers of new credit cards waited in Sarah's mailbox Monday afternoon. Why did she always let it piss her off that she never received a bill? She threw the letters in the recycle bin. Her mortgage, electricity, Internet—everything was sent to her father's accountant, and each clank of the mailbox lid reminded her that she wasn't in control of her own life.

Sure, she'd never really fought for her freedom, but how could she? Growing up learning that she was to be "taken care of" was just like an Australian kid learning to like marmite sandwiches. It was just something you did without question.

Could Chris ever take her seriously? Would a woman as unbelievably together as she was last with someone so…not?

But damn, her feelings for Chris might explode inside her any minute. She'd climbed aboard the rocket and had her finger on the ignition button, wanting more than anything to blast off to that place where love could exist without gravity to slam it back to the ground.

She wanted to be with Chris again. Not just out for another coffee, but to feel her body and taste her and be consumed by her. Yes, she reminded herself, Chris wants to go slower, but the way Chris had kissed her yesterday defied that declaration.

Sarah texted Nat.

I'm about ready to go nuts. Let's go get into trouble.

She closed the laptop.
Her phone buzzed and Nat's answer confused her.

Five-year-old little Johnny was lost...

She was about to reply *WTF* when it buzzed again.

so he went up to a policeman and said, "I've lost my dad!" The policeman said, "What's he like?" Little Johnny replied, "Beer and women."

She laughed. It was Chris. She texted back.

Except for the beer, I'm exactly like little Johnny.

This is probably quite forward of me, but YOU are driving me crazy right now...

Sarah leaned back on the couch, cradling her phone in her lap.

Yeah, well, I'm a mess too.

Figuratively or literally?

Both!

Damn, what the hell am I gonna do with you?

Sarah thought a moment and then typed.

How about we meet in the middle and let me take you somewhere crazy?

I'd like that. I think.

I promise we can have fun without breaking the law.

Okay! When?

What night are you off next?

Tomorrow.

Then tomorrow.

The frustration that had propelled Sarah to text Nat evaporated, as would a hot puff of air into a cooling sky. She'd see Chris again soon, and though her insecurities about whether Chris would feel as much as she already felt scratched at the back of her brain, she was hopeful about the next day.

Nat texted her back and asked her where she wanted to go. Her mind now at ease, she tapped out,

Let's just go get something to eat instead.

❖

Sarah met Natalie at the Nyala Ethiopian Cuisine on Fairfax Avenue. She liked the almost anti-restaurant touches, such as their colorfully painted walls and the custom of eating without utensils.

"This time," Nat said to the waitress, "I'm trying the Yabesha Gommen."

Sarah looked up from her menu. "You know it's made with collard greens, don't you?"

"It's not my favorite veggie, but I always order the same thing, so I'm going for it."

"Good for you," Sarah said, and gave the waitress her order.

Nat waited until the woman walked away. "Are you in a funk?"

"Kind of."

"But you're dating this great gal, and I thought you really liked her."

"I do." Sarah played with the saltshaker. "Chris invited me to a K9 competition. It was really awesome to see what they do. Chris has got it all so together, Nat. But she's worlds apart from me."

"You're getting hung up on the job thing again. Listen, ninety-nine percent of the people you meet are going to have a job. Okay, maybe less in this economy, but why do you insist on letting it be a sticking point? If someone's going to like you, they won't care whether you punch a time clock or not."

"I know, but it always turns out the same. I meet someone and everything's great, but after a while, they start to dislike all the spare time I have, or they feel they can't relate to my life."

"That just means you're not compatible."

"Then I haven't been compatible with every single person I've ever met."

"Well, duh."

"What does that mean?"

"Anyone who's single right now, and that includes me, hasn't found the right one yet."

"At least a lot of you have had long-term relationships. You were with Hailey for six years."

"Six years or six days, it didn't matter. We broke up because it wasn't working out." The waitress came with their drinks, and Natalie ripped open the paper wrapping on her straw. "Six days would have been better. It would have saved me a lot of heartache, I'll tell you."

Sarah understood what Nat was saying, but her life was nothing like Nat's. If it was normal that everyone had baggage,

Sarah felt like she had the entire baggage-claim department at LAX.

"You like her, don't you?"

"A lot."

"More than previous girlfriends?"

"Yes, that's what makes this so scary. I finally feel like I've got something I want so badly that it makes me that much more afraid to lose it."

The waitress brought over their meals.

"This place is so fast." Nat watched the waitress place a plate in front of her, "Thank you."

"Anything else?" the waitress said as she left the bill on the table.

Sarah tore off a piece of injera, but she wasn't hungry. "No, thank you."

"Here." Nat pulled out a credit card and handed it to the waitress. "It's my turn to buy."

The woman picked up the bill and walked away.

"Thanks," Sarah said.

"Listen, Sarah. Don't undermine this. Be honest. I know you aren't sometimes, and it only bites you in the ass."

It would be easier if she had a communicable disease, she thought. At least there were doctors to fix that.

They ate in silence for a while, and when the credit-card receipt came, Nat signed her copy and gave the other to the woman. "May I keep this pen a minute?" The woman shrugged and went back to the kitchen.

Nat turned the receipt over and began to scratch out some lines. "This is you. And this is Chris." She drew two elongated circles close to each other.

"You need to go to art school," Sarah said as she craned her neck to see the image.

"Shut up." Nat drew squiggly lines around the illustrations of them. "This is all the shit you have and this is all the shit she has. And I know she has shit, Sarah, we all do." Another line encircled the ovals and the squiggles. "This is what you need to do."

"Draw crappy portraits of us?"

"I'm gonna fling my collard greens at you." Nat shook the pen at her. "No." She pointed to the drawing. "This outer circle represents you and Chris taking your respective shit and working it all out together. You can't just step out of this circle because you decide it's not going to work. You have to stay in there and give it a real chance."

It was true that in Sarah's past, she was guilty of prematurely ending relationships to avoid the pain of being the one who was broken up with. But then again, she'd also been devastated when she'd tried to stay but then got blindsided by a sudden breakup.

"You talk about stuff," Nat said, "and let her know you want to see where this goes."

"I'm afraid Chris will realize that I'm not the right one, and for once, I don't think I could handle it."

"She may, but maybe she won't." Nat handed her the drawing. "This is your map to find true love."

Sarah looked at it, now right side up. "You just drew a female vajayjay."

Nat glared at her. "You're buying for the next fifty lunches."

❖

"So where are you taking me?"

They were in Chris's SUV, driving down Venice Boulevard toward the Palms District.

"Just a place I figured you'd never go."

"You're making me nervous."

"Because you're not in control?"

"Uh, yeah."

Sarah reached over and took her hand. "Trust me."

Chris was mostly kidding, but a part of her wondered how

far into the grays they were going. Could it be to some sleazy place frequented by undesirables? Or would it be an underground club where the back room dealt in contraband?

She squinted into the bright sun and saw a gray-and-green nondescript building with a brick-colored scroll over the door that read THE MUSEUM OF JURASSIC TECHNOLOGY.

That was a curious name for a museum.

They parked and walked toward the front of the place.

"I didn't know you liked dinosaurs."

Sarah laughed. "You won't find any dinosaurs here."

They stepped in and Sarah said, "This place is dedicated to the advancement of knowledge and the public appreciation of the Lower Jurassic." She grinned mischievously. "But what they mean by the Lower Jurassic is never explained."

They crossed through the foyer and past a slideshow that played what looked like an introduction to the museum. Close by, a plaque hanging on the wall read: *"...the learner must be led always from familiar objects toward the unfamiliar...guided along, as it were, like a chain of flowers into the mysteries of life."*

Chris asked, "What does that mean?"

"It means that the exhibits cross the line between fact and fiction and weave together a fabric of reality and imagination. A lot of critics say that the curators mingle science with art in a way that isn't very museum-like. But that's what I love about this place. It's like they took all the exhibits that no one else wanted because they were too different or didn't fit a standard mold. Instead of following the rules, they do whatever the hell they want here. Come on, let me show you."

They walked past a room whose sign read *NO ONE MAY EVER HAVE THE SAME KNOWLEDGE AGAIN: LETTERS TO MT. WILSON OBSERVATORY.*

"That's where they have a collection of weird letters people have written to the observatory," Sarah said. "It's full of schizophrenic rants and strange proclamations about entrances to other worlds. So cool."

The next exhibit was *THE LIVES OF PERFECT CREATURES: THE DOGS OF THE SOVIET SPACE PROGRAM.* All Chris saw as they went by was an oil-portrait gallery of the cosmonaut canines.

Sarah stopped at another room whose simple sign stated, *THE GARDEN OF EDEN ON WHEELS—SELECTED COLLECTIONS FROM LOS ANGELES AREA MOBILE HOME AND TRAILER PARKS.*

They stepped into a darkened room with small display cases set against the walls. In each case was a miniature vignette of either a mobile home or a travel trailer arranged amidst a forest, a trailer park, or campground setting. All of them glowed and flickered as if tiny people were vacationing or living in each. Sounds of AM radios and televisions played, and Chris could hear crackling campfires and the distant sound of crickets.

The exhibit was purely magical, like she'd been transported, in miniature, to a culture that was on the move and whose roots harkened back to the migratory workers of the Great Depression and the evangelists and salesmen of the 1940s.

She saw Airstream trailers, and canned hams, and even something called a "trailerite" auto camper, set in a scene so flush with flamingos and no-trespassing signs that she could almost hear the cantankerous inhabitant swearing at her from behind the plaid drapes.

These were all distinct, individual statements of fiercely independent souls, of adventurous wanderers, and of capitalistic entrepreneurs, and it all amazed Chris because she'd never seen anything like this place.

They meandered from one display case to the next, talking about the details of each one. The exhibit was surprisingly void of narratives, but there was a complete fluidity throughout, tying everything together, and it allowed them to draw their own conclusions or construct their own critique.

They spent another hour meandering around the maze of

small exhibit rooms looking at specimens and collections, both the beautiful and the bizarre.

"Are you hungry?" Sarah asked after they'd walked out of the museum.

"Starved, actually."

"What do you feel like?"

"I could go for a burger or Mexican."

"How about El Abajeño?"

"Oh, yes! I can taste the carnitas as we speak."

❖

The flat and drab, orange stucco building, displaying signs reading DISCOTECA Y LICORERIA, wasn't particularly inviting, nor would it cause a passerby to stop, but locals knew that big portions of authentic Mexican food awaited them inside.

They ordered and found a table toward the back.

Chris gulped down almost half of her iced tea, and the coolness felt great on her throat. It was another hot day out, and, at one o'clock in the afternoon, the Los Angeles sun was at its most intense.

"That museum was fabulous, Sarah. Thank you for taking me."

"I'm glad you liked it. I wasn't sure at first."

"Well, it wouldn't have been something I'd run to go see, but knowing what it's like, I thought it was really unique. And definitely a gray-area place."

"That's why I picked it. I hoped you'd be interested to see how a place could defy a traditional system and, by its sheer unusualness, create a new way to experience things. It breaks the rules, but in a way that's novel and refreshing."

"I see what you mean. Left to my own choices, I'd have picked the Natural History Museum instead."

"How many times have you been there?"

"Since I was a kid? Probably ten or twelve."

"That's what I mean, a place like that's the rule. I love the exception."

"It's scandalous."

She made Sarah laugh, which pleased her deeply. The more she came to know of her, the more involved her feelings got. And the more time they spent together, the less concerned she was that they'd slept together so soon. Though it was early in their dating, she couldn't imagine being with anyone else. Sarah was her focus now, and she truly wanted to see where this would go.

"Where are you right now?" Sarah said.

"I'm sorry. I was thinking about you and me."

"This may seem presumptuous, but you looked really content just then."

"Well, I can say I'm very glad I craved blackberries that day."

"So, you're happy to be here with me?"

"Very much so. That was the content look I had on my face."

Their food came, and as she dug into her carnitas, Chris said, "What about you?"

"Am I content?"

Chris nodded.

"Right now, yes. Very."

"And in general?"

"I think most people believe that to be content is to put up with whatever state they're in, as when things are sufficient or bearable or when they're moderately happy or satisfied." She rolled up her carne asada burrito a little tighter, not yet taking a bite. "But contentment is so much more than that. It's an inner peace and joy no matter what's happening in your life. Certainly bad things can weigh heavily on your soul, but even in those moments, if you calm yourself down and listen to the silence that is your life, realizations come."

Sarah took a bite, chewing slowly, and Chris realized that

her lips were sexy no matter what she did with them. "Like, what kind of realizations?"

"That the world is a beautiful place. That a stream sounds like God is swishing around, playing in the water. That love is possible, maybe."

"I agree with you," Chris said. "I think happiness comes from events on the outside, but that contentment resides on the inside. Happiness leads to contentment, I suppose. But for me, contentment is the deep breath you take when you've just stepped out of a mountain cabin. The air is crisp and pungent with the smell of pine, and the rustling around you tells you there are perfect little creatures foraging close by, sharing the Earth with you. It tells you that the problems in your day-to-day existence are far, far down the mountain somewhere, but up here, all that matters is the green of the trees and the feel of pebbles under your hiking boots. And the day is yours, to commune with nature, to explore its beauty, to discover yourself in new ways, and to appreciate and pay reverence to your life."

"I think you just painted a picture of contentment for the next publication of the dictionary."

"You also have a very good grasp on life."

"Me?" Sarah looked surprised.

"What you said about finding inner peace and joy, no matter what's happening."

"Most of the time, I don't have a good grasp at all. I know what I want. But making it happen is another thing entirely."

"What do you mean?"

"I've taken so many different classes and tried so many careers, but I never stay with any of them. I don't know who I am and what I want, and that causes me to fail at seeing anything through."

"But you've been with the refuge for a long while."

Sarah's eyes brightened. "I love the refuge. It's my escape."

"So you can't say you don't stay with something."

"The unsticks far outweigh the sticks."

"Well," Chris said, hoping to encourage her, "just focus on what's good about you. And I can tell you, there's a lot."

"You must be referring to my ability to show you a good time."

Chris didn't think Sarah was referring to the night they spent together, but her mind ran all the red lights and drove directly there. "That's probably true. And I'm sure there are lots of other places in L.A. I haven't seen."

"Some of the best places are in Hollywood. Some aren't formal venues, either. What about the neighborhood where the Black Dahlia was found murdered? She was the classic small-town girl with big Hollywood dreams. She had the same thoughts as every girl who shows up here. The field where she was found in the '40s is filled with houses now, but I think it's important to pay homage to the women who come here, as vulnerable as they are hopeful, and so naively entrust their lives to the film machine."

"I think every L.A. cop who wants to be a detective has read about that case."

"And I also go to the apartment building where Sal Mineo was killed. For me, he was so troubled in life and seemed so tormented. One minute, he was on top of the world, starring with James Dean and living an incredibly famous life, and the next, he was out of work and struggling. In the late '60s, he became one of the first major actors in Hollywood to publicly acknowledge his homosexuality, which was extremely brave, but he died at the back of his apartment, and the man who stabbed him didn't even know who he was."

Sarah finally took a bite of her burrito.

"I know those things are morbid," she said, "but they speak to the tragic side of Hollywood. Two people, so full of hope, and giving of themselves to the industry until the rug was brutally pulled out from under them."

Chris studied Sarah as she spoke. She watched her eyes,

which expressed deep feelings for these stories that somehow connected strongly with her.

"You feel a lot, don't you?"

"I suppose I do."

"That's beautiful, Sarah. Although I live in the black-and-white ends of the spectrum, sometimes I think my emotions stay about in the middle. But you seem to experience so much, and so profoundly."

Chris must have hit upon something deep-rooted because Sarah stopped chewing.

After a moment, she said, "When I was a kid, my parents lived close to where I live now. It was up Beachwood Canyon, actually. I was what they called a sensitive child." Her voice faltered a little, as if the words she'd just underscored still hurt. "I would get so upset or sad that I thought if I stayed in the house a minute longer, I'd go crazy. So I'd sneak out and walk up Beachwood, past all the houses. There's a parking lot a ways farther up, and I'd take the trail off of that and climb and climb up to the Hollywood sign. Before 2000, they didn't have a security system to catch those who tried to get to it. It was a hell of a hike, almost straight up at times, but I would finally get to the sign and sit underneath one of the letters. The view's amazing. You can see Catalina Island when it's clear. Sometimes, there'd be a coyote, and I'd watch it roaming through the brush."

She was looking past Chris, probably seeing every bush and rock, and feeling the coastal air sweeping up the hill.

"Anyway," she said, "I'd stay there until I felt better and then I'd hike home."

"Do you still do that?"

"I only go there on the full moon. It's kind of a ritual for me. It's my sanctuary, I guess. But it's harder to get there now. Sometimes it's almost impossible because of the security, but I've found ways."

"I've always wondered if you could get up to the sign."

"It's truly a magical place. Sitting under that icon reminds me of so many dreams and so much hope. Hollywood's a double-edged sword, certainly, but the sign symbolizes the ever-enduring desire for happiness."

"My escape," Chris said, "was to crawl under our porch. We lived in a bungalow, you know, a California Craftsman house. The wooden porch had an access panel on the side, and I'd go in there to get away from all the military orders my parents directed at me. I'd sit there and listen to them ask each other where I was. Then I'd hear my dad clomp out on the porch above me and call my name. It was my way of rebelling. But it wouldn't last long. I'd think about running away, and then images of dead kids, runaway kids that my parents would tell me stories about, would scare the shit out of me. I'd eventually climb back out and toe the line again."

"That sounds as frustrating as my childhood."

"They raised me the way they were raised, and I know they think it was best, but they didn't allow any room for failure. I learned to avoid their displeasure by saluting smartly. You never want to see my father's look of disappointment. It would send you to your knees and paralyze you with terror. I did everything I could to be good for so long, I guess it stuck." Chris looked at her, hoping she'd understand. "That's why I'm a cop now, and that's why I have such a narrow margin for spontaneity and craziness."

A small child in a booth across from them suddenly yelled, "Papa!"

"Ughhh," Sarah suddenly said.

"What's the matter?"

"This coming Sunday."

Chris thought a moment. "Shit. Father's Day."

"Yeah, another rip-roaring good time at the Pullman house."

Chris chuckled. "It can't be as much fun as my parents are."

"Are you going by there?"

"I usually do. I'm off on Sundays, so they expect it."

"I have a proposal for you. If I go with you to your parents' house, will you then come with me to mine?"

"Two sticks in the eye instead of one? Sounds tantalizing."

"That way, we can keep the visits short because of the excuse of needing to visit the other parental unit. Sound like a good time?"

"I'd rather ride a donkey naked through the desert with snapping turtles attached to my nipples, but if I can spend the time with you, I'm all for it."

"Speaking of nipples…"

Chris almost choked on her carnitas. "Yes?"

"Yours are stunning."

A fluttering in her stomach made Chris inhale deeply. "Oh, my God."

"Was that too forward?"

"No! I…I like that you…like them."

"More than like."

Chris tapped her fork against the table. She was aware that Sarah noticed, and even the way she was looking at her now made her want her. Sarah's directness was even sexy. She pulled out her wallet and threw cash on the table. "There's something I need to show you. In the car."

They locked the doors and almost attacked each other. Chris pulled off her shirt and Sarah was right there, pushing her bra aside to take a nipple in her mouth. Her lips and tongue were warm as they sucked and tugged, and she groaned in encouragement of what she was doing.

In the recesses of her mind, the image 647(a) flashed. It was the California penal code for lewd conduct in public. Chris was always on the discovery end of the act, not the active end. But she didn't care right then and pushed it, and all the other warnings, from her mind.

She laid her head back and reached up to hold Sarah's head.

She felt drunk and let the dizziness consume her. One of Sarah's hands moved down and Chris opened her legs. She moaned again, knowing she was already wet.

With her free hand, she began unbuttoning Sarah's shirt, but the angle was challenging. After a few unsuccessful tries, Sarah sat up and helped her.

Chris wasted no time shoving Sarah's shirt aside and pushing her bra up. Taking one nipple in her mouth, she found Sarah so soft and hard and so beautiful she could have changed religions just to worship the goddess who was with her right then.

Sarah shook with little tremors, and her seductive gasps fueled the buzz in Chris's head so much that she had to reach down and unzip Sarah's pants.

A horn suddenly honked and they both jumped. Across the street, a car was blocking another as it tried to exit a driveway.

Chris tried to calm her racing heart while Sarah giggled.

"Fuuuuuck," Chris managed to say when her breathing slowed enough to cough up a word.

She turned back, and the sight of Sarah, exposed and so sensuous, made her sigh.

"God, you're beautiful."

"Who says you're not spontaneous? That's so fucking hot."

Sarah was right. She'd just been extremely impulsive. And that certainly wasn't her at all. She didn't want to think about how risky it had been and that a police officer could have come along, which could be devastating for her. She was with a woman who invigorated her mind and her body, and, for once, she was glad she'd silenced the logical side of her brain.

Sarah handed Chris her shirt and she pulled it on over her head. "After eating Mexican food, I always crave something sweet, but this is a first."

"Hopefully not the last," Sarah said as she buttoned up.

"No, definitely not."

Chapter Ten

Sarah saw Chris almost every night that week. With Chris working until four in the afternoon their schedules matched fairly well. The only challenge was Chris dragging herself out of bed around four thirty to make it to her shift by six. As much as they tried to get to bed early, sleep wouldn't overcome them until much, much later.

So on Friday night, Sarah planned a special date, telling Chris to come over after work and that she would take care of the rest.

When Sarah saw Chris pull into her driveway, a jolt of excitement zipped up her spine and landed on her cheeks, making them flushed and hot. Since meeting Chris, Sarah felt like her life was turning around. She loved spending time with her and felt very secure and happy. On more than a few occasions she'd wake up in the morning with floods of energy and optimism bubbling over inside her. The arrival of junk mail didn't bother her, and she'd even baked bread for her neighbors on either side, chatting with them for the first time in a couple of years.

Chris was a true blessing who invaded her thoughts with promise and possibilities. Whereas she mostly fought the world alone, distrustful of humankind's intentions and dubious of the existence of real happiness, being with Chris rendered those practices and beliefs entirely unnecessary.

Chris was beautiful and funny and attentive in a way that made her consider herself a sacred and precious woman whose thoughts and feelings were valuable instead of a presumed possession that could bestow value. Chris didn't care about the family fortune. She didn't care about using her for sex or for show. Sarah felt an all-embracing and sincere yearning from her that melted the most remote blocks of ice that Sarah knew lurked deep inside her.

Her relationship with Chris was absolutely perfect. And watching Chris get out of her car, Sarah was reminded that being alive was a genuine gift.

She answered the door by pulling Chris in and wrapping her arms around her. They kissed in the foyer, and she could tell by Chris's melodic moans that she was happily surprised.

"I think that was the nicest hello I've ever gotten," Chris said.

"You deserve it." Sarah took her hand and led her to the kitchen. "Drop your keys on the counter. We're taking my car."

"Where are we going?"

"Tonight is your relaxation night, and you'll find out when we get there." Sarah led her out to the garage and hit the automatic door opener. "Now get in the car and our night will begin."

Chris seemed happy to just be with her as they drove toward downtown Los Angeles. They talked about each other's day and the upcoming Father's Day visits that they'd agreed to but then made a vow not to talk anymore about the impending drudgery.

Sarah pulled up to a row of buildings in Koreatown and turned into an alley to park. The almost chaotic variety and abundance of signs, mostly in the vertical Hangul form of the language, made Sarah feel welcomed and immersed in a culture of friendly people, spicy food, traditional music, and a colorful mix of conventional and contemporary fashions.

"Koreatown?" Chris asked as they walked out of the alley and onto the street.

"Yes."

"I'm super curious now."

"Good."

Sarah led her into the Olympic Spa, and Chris's eyes widened.

"Oh, my God. We're getting pampered?"

"Yes, we are."

As they checked in at the front desk in the lobby, Sarah was pleased at the way Chris was looking around like Santa might round the corner any minute.

"The only massage I've ever gotten," Chris said, "was at the mall."

"This is a ladies-only bathhouse. I've heard it's as authentic as it gets."

Two women called matrons came out to greet them, and Chris and Sarah followed them to a room and were instructed to disrobe.

Over the next hour, they were taken to steam rooms and whirlpools, where the soaking of tired muscles commenced. After that, they were treated to scrubs from the matrons in a central trough, and Chris kept peeking over at Sarah, grinning as if she'd just opened the presents Santa had given her in the lobby.

The only conversation between them since arriving came when they were wrapped in cocoon-like quilts and given massages on a heated floor of the nap room.

"I never knew this place was here." Chris's words came out in between gusts of air that the matron was pushing out of her lungs.

"Now you do."

Next came an Akasuri scrub, and Sarah knew the experience of being abraded with Brillo pads would surprise Chris, but she seemed to love the exfoliation.

They were finally taken to a place called the Herbal Hot Pool, which looked like a vat of hot tea.

Sarah watched Chris's eyes widen as she lowered herself in.

"Scalding hot, scalding hot," Chis said quickly as Sarah joined her. Whether the heat put her nerve receptors into shock or the previous treatments had helped desensitize her, it was actually an invigorating soak.

When they eventually got dressed and back out to the car, Chris laid her head back on the seat rest. "I believe I've been polished to a spit shine."

"Your pores will thank you later."

"They already are, and so are my muscles." She lifted her head, her eyes looking so sleepy and adorable. "Thank you so much for tonight."

Sarah started the car. "We're not done yet."

"We're not?"

"No. Just lay your head back again and relax."

❖

Chris awoke when the judder of the car's brakes slowed them down. She'd been aware that they'd been driving a while and tried to make conversation at times, but her body had the structure of a rubber chicken, and Sarah was encouraging her to sleep by rubbing her leg.

She sat up and wiped the drowsiness from her eyes. They were about as far west on Sunset Boulevard as they could be. The curving road was slowing its descent toward the cerulean-blue Pacific Ocean, and Chris couldn't believe she'd been snoozing that long. "We're in Pacific Palisades."

"Yes, we are," Sarah said as she pulled into a driveway of a rather large complex.

SELF-REALIZATION FELLOWSHIP, LAKE SHRINE. WELCOME TO THESE MEDITATION GARDENS. When Chris read the sign aloud it sounded almost comical. "When anyone mentions Sunset Boulevard, I think about celebrities and mansions, not inner peace and meditation."

"L.A. is all about finding interesting things where they're least suspected," Sarah said as she parked. "Can you walk?"

Chris laughed. "I'm not sure, but if you have a blanket, you can just pull me behind you."

What Chris saw first was a beautiful temple, probably six stories high and sitting on a hill. The construction and details looked both Eastern and Western, but its domed octagonal shape, crowned with a stunning golden lotus, reminded her more of India than anywhere else.

Sarah took her hand as they entered the temple, and they stopped just inside the doors. The open span of the domed ceiling was painted white, and the temple was lined with pews facing a simple altar. Minimal but magnificent decorative pieces of stained glass and woodcarvings were interspersed around the stark whiteness of the plaster walls, conveying a royal but humble ambiance.

"The court outside honors the five principal religions of the world. And a memorial over there holds a portion of Mahatma Gandhi's ashes."

"This place is beautiful," Chris said as the solitude enveloped her mushy-muscled body.

"George Harrison's memorial service was held here."

"That makes perfect sense," Chris said, picturing the bearded Beatle happily strumming a ukulele as he floated above those gathering in his honor.

"Come here," Sarah said, leading her out. "The best is in back."

Chris was dumbfounded that this gorgeous lake and thick vegetation sat right off Sunset Boulevard. She had to have driven down this road a thousand times, and she'd been mere feet away.

The lake and surrounding gardens had to comprise at least ten acres. Trees and flowers seemed to hug the water, and the foliage was so unique, it was as if they'd all had their passports stamped with happy faces upon arriving in the United States from their own special corners of the world. Swans floated on the water, cleaning their plumage, as koi, ducks, and multitudes of turtles communed with waterfalls, statues, and fern grottos.

A Mississippi paddleboat and a Danish windmill were the only two unexpected structures sitting on the edge of the lake, but even they seemed appropriate and serene in this context.

Chris and Sarah stood at the edge of the lake, not saying anything for a while until Chris squeezed Sarah's hand. "I can't believe how peaceful it is here. I forget there's even traffic on the other side of those walls."

"Do you like it?"

"I really do."

"Let me take you to my favorite place here."

They walked around the edge of the lake and then veered off on a brick path to an alcove tucked away among some trees. A marble bench awaited them as they sat on the seat, cool in the shade.

"I come here sometimes to unwind," Sarah said. "Natalie brought me here for the first time. She'd never admit it to you, but she's a huge Elvis fan, and he used to come here a lot."

Chris laughed. "It seems like a long way from *Viva Las Vegas.*"

"So true." Sarah joined her with a giggle. "I guess he needed a place to get away, like everyone else."

"Thank you for taking care of me today. This is one of the best places I could ever imagine." Chris put her arm around Sarah. "And I'm with the best woman I could ever imagine."

Sarah kissed her, and Chris could feel a thousand angels warming her heart with the serenity of the moment. She also felt pure joy.

CHAPTER ELEVEN

Chris and Sarah pulled up to a modest ranch-style house in El Toro. It had a severely trimmed lawn with tight, square hedges and was painted in perfunctory gray with white trim.

"This is Casa Bergstrom," Chris said as she drove past and found a spot a few houses down.

"There's room in the driveway."

"Not for a car that might leak oil."

Sarah already felt her nerves tense in anticipation.

Chris let herself in, and as they walked toward the back, Sarah saw a front room as tightly manicured as the front lawn. Practical furniture, arranged neatly, created a square space sitting perfectly arranged around a gray area rug whose borders looked as if the furniture would pay dearly if they dared to cross over.

As they passed through, Sarah noticed that the bookcase was filled with books organized in order of size. And color.

As they entered the kitchen, Chris whispered, "Assume the position."

Three people looked her way, and Chris introduced Sarah.

"Mother, Father, Jeb, this is Sarah Pullman."

Chris's father shook her hand, and her mother, who was stirring something in a bowl, said hello. Chris's brother nodded.

"May I get you something to drink?" Chris's father said to Sarah.

"Wine would be nice."

Chris's mother stopped stirring and looked at her father.

"We have water or soda," her father said as he walked toward the refrigerator.

"Water is fine." Though it would make the night a lot longer.

Throughout the next half hour, Sarah listened to the small talk among the Bergstroms and occasionally answered questions. She was very familiar with the trivial diatribe and knew she'd be in the middle of the same later.

Sarah told them she worked at the wildlife refuge but didn't say that she wasn't paid. They seemed to be interested in the organization, so maybe that was good.

Dinner of chicken with mashed potatoes and peas went fairly well, if one considered the ability of the entire family to spread the topics of weather, sports, and Jeb's job at the army base throughout the entire affair without a smile or even a nod.

"How's Abel?" Chris's father asked as her mother cleared the dishes.

"He's great. I haven't gotten many bites, but I also haven't had to tackle any bad guys in a while."

"Are you keeping in shape?"

Sarah wanted to say that Chris was in fine shape the nights they'd spent together but bit her tongue.

"Yes, sir."

"When are you planning to test for the sergeant's position?"

"I don't know if I will. I'd have to give up the K9 unit, and I'd rather not have to deal with more station time and paperwork."

"You need to plan for retirement, Chris. That's mission critical. Climbing the ranks puts more PERS in your pocket."

Chris leaned toward Sarah and said, "That's the public employees' retirement system. It's our pension and health benefits program." She turned back to her father. "I may take the test in the future, but for right now, I like what I'm doing."

"The future has a way of sneaking up behind you and biting you in the ass."

That's what Abel's for, Sarah thought.

She didn't like that Chris looked down at her plate, but she did come back fairly quickly.

"Remember when I told you about the call I went on where a man had run into a lake?" Chris said to her father. "We couldn't see him at all, and Abel led us to the place he'd jumped in. And remember when I found him underwater, not breathing, and resuscitated the guy?"

"I do," he said.

"The mayor's office is giving me a lifesaving award for that."

"You've been on the force ten years. It's about time. Good."

It hurt Sarah to see Chris's disappointment. She too had felt the sting of the classic slap and tickle from her parents. She reached under the table and found Chris's hand, squeezing it. She got a squeeze back, but it was weak with what had to be disenchantment.

They got out of the house without further disparagement, and Sarah put her arm around Chris as they walked to the car. "Your mother didn't say much of anything throughout dinner."

"That's her way of surviving the marriage."

"It's sad to have to survive anything," Sarah said, and the truth of her statement made her throat tighten in empathy.

They got in the car and Chris started the engine. Sarah put her hand on Chris's. "Are you okay? We don't have to go to my parents' now. It won't be any more fun, and I think you've had enough laughs for today."

Chris kissed her gently. "Listen, I'm glad to have served my tour of duty at Casa Bergstrom, so anything after that is like child's play."

"Don't be so sure," Sarah said, and made a funny face when Chris looked at her.

❖

Chris pulled into the rather tony neighborhood of Bel Air. The street wound up a hill that seemed to have been commanded—by all the moneyed residents—to rise only gradually for their own private, overindulged convenience.

Sarah directed her into a circular driveway that served as a dramatic introduction to a house so grand and antebellum in style that Chris expected Colonel Sanders to be standing on the steps, awaiting their arrival.

Large columns held up the three-story, neoclassical plantation house, and a magnificent double entry would impress even the most jaded Hollywood celebrities.

"Did you ever live here?" Chris asked as they walked up the main steps.

"Only for a few years. We moved here from the Hollywood Hills when I was fourteen, and I vacated the premises when I was eighteen. I hated this place. We had to give the movers a map of the place so they wouldn't get lost. It's too big and too garish for me."

Piano music and loud voices greeted them as soon as Sarah opened the door. Visible through a living room full of people drinking and talking, a man in a black shirt and pants played the piano with arm movements so exaggerated the overtly flamboyant song sounded horribly ostentatious.

Judging by the look on Sarah's face, this whole scene seemed to be a surprise.

"What the fuck?" Sarah said as they stepped through the foyer.

Clearly a cocktail party was under way, and it reminded Chris of something out of a sixties movie. Most people just turned and smiled as they walked through the living room, and one or two whispered to each other, obviously sharing some tidbit about Sarah.

More people clustered in a den whose centerpieces were a mahogany desk, overstuffed easy chairs, and a fireplace that looked to be made from lava rock. Sarah targeted a man and woman standing by a rather large urn.

"What's going on?"

The man turned to her. "Sarah. I'm glad you could make it."

"Who are all these people?"

"Colleagues and investors."

"It's Father's Day. Doesn't that mean we have a quiet dinner instead of a networking event?

"Sarah, honey." The woman next to him spoke, and Chris assumed it was Sarah's mother. "It's both. Your father has a joint-venture meeting tomorrow, and this is important."

Sarah just shrugged and then introduced Chris to her parents. "This is Chris." She turned to Chris. "This is Charles and Sharon."

"Where's Grandma?" Sarah said.

Charles used his drink to gesture behind Sarah. "In the library."

Without saying anything else, Sarah took Chris's hand and led her away.

"You call your parents by their first names?"

"They haven't been my parents for a long time."

The library was a testament to the art of woodcrafting. Floor-to-ceiling bookcases stood like sentries, holding so many books, the collection would make a librarian swoon.

A thin, delicate woman sat in a large upholstered chair. Her features were pinched, but her beauty had endured the years. She looked up from a book. "Sarah!"

Greeting her with a long hug, Sarah whispered something and then introduced them.

"Grandma, this is Chris. And Chris, this is Momo, the best grandma in the world."

They sat in a couch that cornered the chair. The atmosphere in the room was very calm, so different from where they'd just been, and Chris could easily see the genuine love between Sarah and her grandmother. The tense ambiance of impatience and hostility they'd just waded through was absent.

"It's very nice to meet you," Chris hesitated, hoping she'd remembered her name correctly, "Momo."

"It's Norwegian," Momo said. "Short for Mormor, the name for a mother's mom." She reached out and Sarah took her hand. "So, how have you been, my darling?"

"Things have been good."

"I heard about the fire at the refuge on television. Is everything okay?"

"It is, Momo. Chris even helped evacuate the animals."

She turned to Chris. "You're a good girl."

An odd sensation lulled her, exposing a vulnerable spot of basic human need in a way that warm hands reach toward you and pull you in from the cold. She suddenly couldn't remember if her parents had ever said something as simple and affirming.

"…that you do?"

Chris blinked. "I'm sorry, Momo, what were you saying?"

"What is it that you do?"

"I'm a police officer here in Los Angeles."

"A civil servant protecting all of us. That's noble and courageous."

That vulnerable feeling came over her again, and she cleared her throat. "Thank you."

The door of the library opened and Mrs. Pullman came in, along with the sound of the piano music.

"Sarah, come out and mingle, please."

"I'm visiting with Momo."

"She'll be here after the party. It's your father's day today."

"I would venture to guess that it's father's day every day."

Her father stepped in, drink still in his hand. "Sarah, you're being rude to our guests. I'd like them to see you interacting."

"I'll be there in a while."

"It's just like you, never carrying through." He almost

sloshed the alcohol out of his glass. "You spend five seconds out there and then run and hide."

"I'm not going to get into this, Charles."

"Oh, I agree, you don't get into anything. You're really good at doing something for a while, but then you never carry through."

"Seriously, are you really going to do this?"

Mrs. Pullman touched his arm. "Let's get you another drink, Charles."

He looked at Sarah as if she'd burned the house down. The silence in the room almost screamed. Finally, Sarah's parents left.

Sarah's anger had congealed quickly, and she said in a mocking tone, "Yeah, Charles, have another drink."

Momo must have squeezed her hand because Sarah abruptly turned to her. "You're out on your own now, Sarah. You don't have to listen to him. My damn son-in-law has his own self to blame for trying to force the family into such a narrow margin. You should have had a better father."

"I'm sorry," Sarah said to her. "You were enjoying such a calm evening, and I just flew you into some turbulence."

"I'm used to the hurly-burly, my darling."

Chris thought that was about the cutest thing she'd heard in a long time.

"I wish you'd come live with me," Sarah said. "We could be two crazy girls on our own."

That got a laugh out of Momo. "We could sure raise the roof, huh? But then who would give your father the business?"

"I sure love you, Momo."

"And I love you, my darling Sarah." She patted Sarah's hand before releasing it. "I'm just about at a part in this book where there's going to be a scrumptious murder," Momo said with a definite gleam in her eye. "You go ahead and see your father so he doesn't blow a carburetor, or whatever it is that gets blown."

Chris stood when Sarah did. "Okay. But I'll be by soon to see you."

She kissed her grandmother and stepped aside.

Chris took Momo's hand. "It was a pleasure to meet you."

"I feel the same way. Now, you two make an appearance and then go have fun somewhere else."

As they left the library, Chris said, "When we first went in there, what did you whisper to her?"

Sarah's expression could have come straight from an elf revealing a heavily guarded secret he'd overheard from Santa. "I said to her, 'She's one of the good ones.'"

Chris stopped and pulled her in for a kiss. It was a thank you of sorts but was also in empathy of what she felt, having to endure many of the same familial issues that she had lived through in her own home.

"That's just dandy." Mr. Pullman stood a few feet away with a group of people. "What else would you like to do for your dear old dad on Father's Day?"

Chris tensed up immediately and held her breath. As fast as a music video montage, visions of various domestic-violence calls flipped through her mind. Instinct told her to be ready. If a flashpoint came she'd tug hard on Sarah's hand and pull her away.

Sarah's hand slid into hers.

"Jesus, Father," was all Sarah said, and it was Chris who was being pulled away toward the door. The fifteen or so feet they walked before exiting the house seemed like a mile. And the whole way, she could have sworn that the showy piano man was playing the same pretentious riff.

"I hate it when people drink to excess," Sarah said when they got back in the car. "I see the binges coming on and I just want to scream."

"Are you all right?" Chris asked.

Sarah's laugh was so unexpected it startled her. "I'm sorry,"

Sarah said, "but do you know I said the exact same thing to you when we left your parents' house?"

"You did."

"How did we survive?"

"Our families," Chris said, "aren't too dissimilar. I became a lot like my parents because that's how I figured I could gain their acceptance. You became the opposite so you wouldn't succumb."

Sarah stayed silent, but Chris knew she was chewing on those family bones.

"I dwell in the extremes," Chris said, "and function within the absolutes of right and wrong, and you live in the grays and see the world in all its contradictory forms."

"We're kind of fucked up, aren't we?"

"God, I hope to hell not!"

"Shit, this wasn't such a good idea, was it?"

"In a way, it was. I understand more about who you are."

"And I understand where you get your ironing abilities." She saluted as a teasing grin formed.

"Ironing?"

"I've never seen a wrinkle on you. I bet you can bounce a dime off your bed."

"What makes you think my bed isn't sitting there completely unmade."

"I don't think so."

"Damn."

"It's made, isn't it?"

"Yes."

Their laughter helped ease the tension they'd absorbed at the parental-home visits. They had been equally uncomfortable, but the experience had drawn her closer to Sarah. It was like they'd shared a foxhole and come out of the artillery assault relatively unscathed.

Here they were, having endured each other's family secrets,

and after the initial discomfort, Chris was hit with a rush of intimacy. Sarah was a strong, beautiful woman, and Chris's thoughts wasted no time wandering to what lay beneath Sarah's clothes. And the lips that were now formed in the shape that laughter brings had done amazing things to her. Her brain then dispatched a vise that tightened the space between her legs. To hell with convention, she decided.

Chris started the car. "Do you happen to have a dime?"

❖

Chris and Sarah fell onto Chris's bed, rumpling the perfectly stretched sheets.

She kissed Sarah slowly, then passionately. She turned her around, running her hands over her stomach, hips, breasts, as Sarah sighed.

Sarah complied easily as Chris bent her over at the waist. Sarah's hands found the bed, and Chris grabbed hold of her hips and bowed down until her chest met Sarah's back. She kissed Sarah's shirt, pulling it up with her teeth until her lips could feel the warm skin of her back.

Chris knew she was on autopilot but wouldn't take over the controls. She wanted Sarah so much that making love to her didn't even seem like enough. A forceful ache almost moved her to tears because she wanted to worship her. Every cell in her being wanted to protect her and keep her safe.

She reached around and unzipped Sarah's pants, letting them slide to the floor, and groaned when Sarah's hips pushed into hers. She quickly kicked her shoes and pants off her feet.

As soon as she slipped Sarah's underwear off, she turned her around and knelt in front of her. She tasted the wet spot between Sarah's legs, and a dizzying feeling spun even more wildly when she felt the grip of Sarah's hands on her hair.

Chris looked up to see Sarah's head falling back and her chest heaving up and down.

Sarah sucked in a breath and moaned loudly.

"God," Sarah said. "I want you inside me."

Chris wanted her, too. Her legs, her arms, her mouth. She wanted her entirely.

She stood quickly and heard a sexy whimper come from Sarah. Laying her back on the bed, Chris undressed quickly, hardly taking her eyes off Sarah, who now removed her top and bra.

Chris's need pulled strongly as she lay down next to Sarah. Nuzzling her nose in Sarah's hair, she felt completely whole.

She kissed her neck as Sarah's hands wrapped around her, and soon, Sarah's breathing increased and Chris felt Sarah's hands upon her shoulders, urgently tugging her down.

"Please," Sarah said.

Chris's tongue explored her body, leaving a wet trail as she made her way down, across her clavicle, around both breasts, playfully sucking and biting, and then lavishing herself on Sarah's belly. There was a slight lift, just under her belly button, that allowed her tongue to ride up and over, like a leaf that flows on a current.

Her hair was being pulled down again, and Chris's pulse quickened. Sarah wanted her even more now, so she didn't linger any longer on that fabulous stomach.

Chris kissed the insides of her thighs, and Sarah responded by spreading her legs. Chris ran her tongue down her thigh, tasting the sweetness of her skin, and arrived at the underside of her knee. She was hot to the touch and softer than the petals of a fresh red rose.

Sarah's fingers tickled Chris's cheeks and drew her up, helping her mouth find the wettest place Chris could imagine.

Sarah arched her back, pushing into Chris's mouth, and moaned a sultry melody just for her. In appreciation, Chris swirled her tongue, finding the sensitive places that would make Sarah twitch and grab her hair more firmly.

Sarah began to shake as her clit hardened under Chris's

tongue. Her moans grew louder, so Chris wrapped her arms underneath Sarah's thighs and held her tighter.

In a building crescendo, Sarah moved against Chris's mouth in increasing circles, almost rising off the mattress. Chris stayed with her, devoted to the pleasure she wanted so much to give, and suddenly, Sarah's body tensed.

She called out Chris's name and came in her mouth, the waves of contractions squeezing her chin. When she eventually slid up Sarah's still-shaking body, Chris felt overwhelmed with affection and caring and wrapped her arms tightly around her. The trembling that originated deep inside her juddered and quivered without warning. She was overcome with emotion so potent that she was afraid it might explode inside her. It both excited and frightened her.

"My God," Sarah said, and gently kissed Chris's cheek, and lips, and eyes.

Chris exhaled a breath she'd held a little too long. "Yeah."

Sarah leaned back ever so slightly and looked at her. "I have no words."

Chris kissed her. "I know what you mean."

"Are you okay with this?"

"Yes." And Chris truly meant it. "I'm beginning to forget why I wanted to slow things down."

"Sometimes crossing a line can be pretty scary. I understand why you felt that way before."

"Has any of this been scary for you?"

For a moment, it seemed that Sarah's mind floated away because she looked toward the ceiling and the muscles in her face fell ever so faintly. In a nanosecond, she appeared sad, and then the expression vanished.

"Being with you isn't scary at all. It's like I've been underwater too long, flailing around, and a hand reached down to pull me up. And as I take my first gulp of air, I realize the hand is yours."

"That's beautiful, Sarah."

Sarah was nose to nose with her. "And so are you."

Chris felt the heat from her mouth right before their tongues touched. Everything about her set Chris ablaze. It was as if a colossal underground oil deposit was on fire. There was heat everywhere and no apparent way to put it out.

Sarah put her head on Chris's shoulder.

"If I may step into presumptuousness here," Chris said, "I believe we might be racing toward becoming an item."

"You are stepping into it," Sarah said, "and I don't see any bullshit on your shoes."

Chris laughed. "That's a nice picture."

"So is this."

Chris looked down and watched Sarah's hand trace a path toward her stomach.

"You know," Sarah said, "I felt you do things with your mouth that ruined any memories I have of anyone else."

"I take that as a good thing?"

"You should."

"Good, because that comment could have gone either way."

"It was definitely meant in the right way."

"I don't know what it is about you," Chris held her tighter, "but you make me think crazy things."

"Like what?"

"Like, I want to run down to the supermarket and put enough quarters into the candy machine until I get one of those temporary tattoos, the one that looks like a heart with arrows through it, and stick it on my chest."

"That's adorable."

"And I want to change my Facebook status, like, right now." Chris stopped, suddenly afraid she might have pushed things too far. She didn't know if that remark had frightened Sarah, but quite frankly, that declaration, so abrupt and so unlike her, was terrifying the shit out of her.

Sarah didn't say anything right away, and prickles of anxiety and regret started to erupt under Chris's skin.

"Shit, that was too much, wasn't it?" Chris damned herself. "I'm sorry if that scared you."

"It didn't."

She looked at Sarah but couldn't read the emotion just under the surface of her smile.

"It didn't," Sarah said again. "It's just that…"

Chris held her breath, expecting something bad, like a kid anticipating a painful tetanus shot.

"You were right to want to go slowly. We don't know each other that well."

"Are you regretting…this?"

"No, not at all. It's just that you're a wonderful, honest, and amazing woman. And now you've met my family, so you know what kind of upbringing I had." She lifted her hand to Chris's cheek. "But there's so much you don't know about me."

"And there's a lot you don't know about me, as well."

"That's true."

"I mean, some parts of me might scare you into tomorrow."

That distant expression washed over Sarah's face again. Chris felt pangs of compassion for Sarah because so much seemed to dwell deep down inside her.

"I've experienced the worst," Sarah finally said. "So nothing scares me anymore."

"Are you warning me about something?" Whatever it was, Chris couldn't imagine it being so bad that she'd change her mind about anything.

"No, I'm saying that I screw things up."

"We all do."

"There are things you don't know about my past."

"What could be so bad?"

Sarah wouldn't answer.

"Have you committed any felonies?"

"No."

"Have you killed anyone?"

"Of course not."

"Then whatever it is, I think the operative word, here, is *past*."

"You saw my parents. They like the fact that they have children to talk to their friends about, but other than that, I was just an issue to be dealt with." Sarah paused. "I remember, when I was in, maybe, sixth grade, I found a word in the dictionary, and it seemed that, with that one word, I understood my whole life, like its meaning had just been defined."

"What was it?"

"*Chattel*. It said something like, an item of movable personal property, such as furniture." Sarah paused. "Or me. Old Charles and Sharon moved me around at their convenience. To show off their little creations, they placed me in the middle of cocktail parties. When they wanted to enjoy the summer, they shipped me off to places like a social-economics camp."

"What the heck is that?"

"I can tell you that my days weren't filled with swimming and campfire stories but courses in business-plan writing, with a *sporting* competition at the end, of course, and learning about for-profit and non-profit businesses."

"Are you kidding?"

"I wish I was. And when I'd get home, they guaranteed I wouldn't get in the way of their lives by keeping all of us upstairs in our rooms and watched over by the servant staff, who stayed at the top of the stairs making sure we wouldn't be seen."

"Did they do that to your sister and brother as well?"

"Yeah. My sister's a lot older and was the well-behaved one. She'd send herself off to camps and was only around when they asked. I'm sure it was her way of avoiding them. And my brother didn't seem to care one way or the other. No wonder my sister is now married to an asshole and my brother does more drugs than he sells."

"I'm so sorry, Sarah."

"So, after I saw that word in the dictionary, I remember yelling at my mother, telling her I knew what they were up to and that even chattel have feelings."

"Oh, Sarah."

"A shrink once told me, 'Something breaks the mind and the will of anyone so stripped of autonomy.'"

Chris's heart hurt so badly for her. A flood of pain seemed to be inside Sarah that was constantly seeping over the edges of the dam. She held her tighter, kissing her forehead.

"Oh, God, listen to me. I've become a bummer."

"You are not a bummer. I'm glad you told me all that."

Sarah drew in a big breath and let it out. "One of the greatest days of my life is when I became an adult and moved out. I try to think of my whole childhood as a badly scripted television show whose only saving grace was that it got canceled. But even so, whenever I go home I'm still in a series of reruns."

Chris kissed her. "I'm really digging who you've become."

"Yeah?"

"Yeah. You've got a brilliant mind, you make me laugh, and you're sexy as hell."

Sarah's face brightened, which pleased Chris like nothing else.

"Well," Sarah said as she rolled on top of Chris. "I think I owe you something for those compliments."

"You don't—" Sarah's incredibly sexy lips on Chris's stifled her words. And shortly after she felt those amazing hips moving against hers, her mind went happily blank.

CHAPTER TWELVE

Sarah arrived at the refuge first thing Monday morning. Madeleine was inside mostly, still keeping an eye on the news. She'd come out every once in a while to update the volunteers, and so far, the only blaze the reporters were following was in Topanga Canyon, too far away to worry about.

Sarah spent the first few hours walking the perimeter fences, looking for broken or worn spots. Having repaired a few, she was now cooling off from the intense midday sun with two frozen fruit pops—one for her and one for Sasha. They sat almost next to each other, with the fence in between them, slurping on the frozen cherry-juice-and-raisin treat.

"I guess it is possible to have a normal life," she said as Sasha concentrated on her frozen delicacy, only glancing up once. "I mean, at some point, you just move on, right?"

Sasha's reply came in wet smacks.

"You seem to be doing okay, right? You've become the matriarch of your tribe and you seem happy." Sarah finished her pop and stared at the stick. "I just don't want to fuck it up."

Sasha looked up at her.

"Sorry. *Mess* it up." She licked a fruity drip that was threatening to fall. "You just do your thing, don't you? You wake up every day and do what you need to do."

She waited in case Sasha might decide to answer.

"I guess that's good advice for me. Nothing can change the past. You simply take a step forward and don't worry about what's behind you, huh?"

❖

On her way home, Sarah decided to stop by Chris's and surprise her. She imagined the look on her face, so adorable and happy. Maybe they'd just watch TV or order food online, and perhaps she'd spend the night.

It was after dark and Chris had been off for a couple of hours. She stopped by the store to pick up some ice cream. She wasn't sure if Chris would like Rocky Road, but didn't everyone? Who could not love little bits of nuts and marshmallows swimming in an ocean of chocolate?

Sarah could hear faint music inside Chris's house and rang the doorbell. She listened for a minute but couldn't hear much else. She rang again.

The doorknob rattled, as if stuck, and then the door swung open.

"I brought..." Sarah's mouth dropped open.

Chris wobbled and grabbed the doorframe. It seemed a struggle for her to focus. It wasn't hard to put the pieces together.

"Are you drunk?"

"Yup."

"What's wrong? What happened?"

Chris turned around and lost her balance, catching herself by shuffling her feet as if she were a football player sidestepping a tackle. Sarah followed her inside and closed the door.

"Chris," Sarah said, but Chris walked into the kitchen without saying anything. What was going on? She'd never seen her drink alcohol, let alone get smashed.

"Chris," Sarah repeated, and stopped just inside the kitchen door when Chris bumped against the counter, turned around, and held a finger up.

"Not a good time," Chris said, and reached for a bottle of Scotch that sat close by. The cap was already off and it was about a third empty.

"What's going on?"

"What's going on," she said, waving the bottle as if she were underlining her words, "is a shitty end to a shitty day."

"What happened?"

Chris just looked down and shook her head.

"Chris, please." Sarah stepped toward her.

"It's just fucked up."

"What's fucked up?"

Chris raised her head, and the look of pain on her face hit Sarah in the stomach. She wondered if Abel was okay, if someone had been killed, if Chris had gotten into trouble. Not knowing what had happened was excruciating.

"A call I went on today," Chris finally said. "I backed up a rookie officer on a DV—"

"DV?"

"Domestic-violence call. The man that answered the door didn't want to let us in, but we could hear the woman behind him. She sounded okay, but Perkins, my partner, told the man he needed to check on her anyway. The man said he didn't understand why we needed to come in, and all of a sudden, Perkins smashed the door open in the guy's face. He charged in and tackled the guy. He shouldn't have done that. I had Abel with me, and the whole time Perkins was punching him, I was making sure the woman wasn't going to run into another room and get a gun or something. I mean, he went berserk on the guy for no reason, and we hadn't even cleared the house.

"Perkins had the guy against a couch, kicking the shit out of him. He handcuffed the guy, and I kept watching the woman while he finally cleared the house. So then, the guy was sitting on the ground in handcuffs and said something like, 'Why'd you punch me?' and Perkins went over and punched the guy again, screaming at him that he was gonna fuck him up even more."

Chris ran her hand roughly through her hair. "He can't do that. The guy was handcuffed. Perkins is a rookie, but he knows he can't do that."

"That's what upset you?"

Chris's chuckle sounded miserable. "No. Sergeant Shaffer showed up. He has it in for me."

"Why?"

"He was once a K9 handler and got kicked off the team. I was the next officer to get a dog, and he's been pissed ever since. He eventually got promoted and still spends a lot of time riding my ass."

"What happened then?"

"Perkins had already put the man in his squad car, so I took the woman outside and put her in Sergeant Shaffer's car. When I walked back in, I saw Shaffer pick up a knife that was on a bookcase and walk it over to the couch where the man had been. He put it under the cushion and said to the rookie, "Well, look what we found here. That guy was going for a knife. That's cause for you to do what you did while he was cuffed.'

"Then he turned to me and started screaming at me about why I didn't put Abel on the guy. He was yelling that an officer was in need of assistance and I didn't do a damn thing."

"Oh, my God."

"I finally said to him that the situation didn't merit the extra force and left it at that." Chris exhaled loudly, clearly distressed and still reliving each second.

"When the sergeant left, I ripped the rookie a new one and told him he'd better tell the truth in his report because that's what I was going to do."

"Do you think he will?"

"I don't know. All I do know is that the whole department is going to think I didn't back my partner up."

"But you said you couldn't because you were watching the woman. Jesus, Chris, that guy Perkins had tunnel vision and could have gotten shot in the head."

"I know."

"And you're gonna get your name drug through the mud because of Sergeant Shaffer?"

"I've never seen a cop do anything dirty. He planted that knife and told the rookie to lie."

"That's why you started to drink?"

Chris nodded.

"Can you tell anyone? Someone higher in rank than the sergeant?"

"I don't know what I'm going to do. That's what's so fucked up." Chris reached for the bottle again and took a swig.

"Don't you think you've had enough?"

"What?" Chris suddenly yelled. "Enough to erase what I saw? Not yet."

"Okay." Sarah raised her hands, trying to defuse her anger.

"No, it's not okay! It's supposed to be black and white. *Black and fucking white!*" She stopped shouting and just stared at a spot on the wall somewhere over Sarah's left shoulder. "Right and wrong. That's the code. We go after the wrongs. We don't create them. Anyone who watches TV knows what a dirty cop is. I've just never seen one until tonight."

Chris was shattered by what had happened, but it shocked Sarah to see what she'd done to herself because of it.

"It's so fucked," Chris said again.

"Chris," she said carefully, "is this why I've never seen you drink?"

Another miserable laugh came from Chris, and Sarah wondered if she might start yelling again.

"So, you've found my demon," Chris said. "Yes, I drink

sometimes. It's a way to handle being perfect all the fucking time. Or, at least, it's a way to deal with the fact that I'm not."

"But you didn't do anything wrong tonight."

"It doesn't matter. The department is going to lose trust in me. I'm sure the sergeant is telling everyone right now that I just stood there while Perkins needed help."

"But your report will explain it."

"I've had more from him than I can take. Every night, he's on the radio talking to me like I'm some idiot or telling other officers what I did wrong on this bite call or that bite call. It's grating me to fucking death." She slid down until she was sitting on the floor and dropped her head to her knees.

Sarah knelt down and put her arms around her. "You're right. It is fucked. And it's not fair."

"Could you just go, please?"

"Why?"

"I don't want company right now."

"Chris—"

"Please," she said, louder this time.

Sarah was well rehearsed at dealing with drunken parents. It was virtually a family pastime. She hated it then and really didn't like it now.

Chris raised her head, glaring at Sarah. "I've handled myself all my life. I know what I'm doing. So you can go home now."

"So you like drinking yourself into a stupor."

"If I want to, yes!" she yelled, startling Sarah. "Fuck. I don't feel good."

Chris began to stand and Sarah helped her up. If she hadn't steered her toward the bathroom, Chris wouldn't have made it to the toilet before throwing up.

"Please leave," Chris said in between retches.

Sarah got a washcloth and ran it under the faucet. She leaned against the counter until Chris was through.

"Ughhh," Chris finally said.

Sarah leaned over and pulled Chris's hair up to place the washcloth on her neck. "Do you need to throw up again?"

"I don't think so."

"Do you want to lie down now?"

Chris nodded, so Sarah helped her up and took her to her room. With her shoes off and a grumble that she wanted the rest of her clothes on, Chris climbed into bed. Sarah fetched a trash can and put it on the floor next to the bed and then got a glass of water.

"Thank you," Chris said before she fell asleep.

Sarah lay down next to her, and when Chris didn't awake for a couple of hours, she got up and stood over her. Sarah felt so much for Chris and was beginning to understand her more. She didn't like the aggression that alcohol brought out, but she knew better than anyone that nobody is completely free from transgressions. Still, this behavior was way too close to home. Her fuse had been cut short long ago.

They needed to have a serious conversation about this, but for now, she was glad Chris was safe. She just wished she could help her with her struggles at work.

"So, you have an Achilles's heel like everyone else," she said to Chris, who was snoring lightly. "That just makes you more human."

She kissed her on the forehead and let herself out.

❖

Momo didn't look that well, Sarah thought as she walked into the library Tuesday morning. She'd stopped by, glad her parents were gone, and found her grandmother sitting with a book in her hands; however, she wasn't reading. Instead, she stared out the window as if watching something that was more interesting than the text in front of her.

"Whatcha doing, Momo?"

She turned and smiled at her. "Sarah, my darling. I was just thinking about your grandfather."

"What about him?"

"I remember mornings with him when I would get up early to make coffee, and then he'd come out into the kitchen and tell me how wonderful his good morning smelled. He said that when he got a whiff of the coffee brewing, he knew I loved him."

"That's wonderful." She sat down on the couch. "Are you feeling all right?"

"I suppose. I didn't sleep well last night."

"Can I get you anything?"

"No, my darling. Just seeing you is the best medicine."

"And I can say the same about you."

"Tell me, how is your new girl?"

"Chris? She's great." There was no need to tell her about the night before. She hoped Chris's overindulgence was a one-time thing and wouldn't affect their relationship, but every bit of experience told her it wasn't.

"That's good to hear. And how are the animals?"

Sarah didn't have anywhere to be that day, so she happily settled in to give her an update on Sasha and the rest of the animals and people at the refuge.

❖

Chris walked through the station, aware that any of the officers could be talking about her. She hadn't yet heard a thing, but she was still raw from the DV call, and the jackhammering in her head reminded her of how she'd handled it.

She didn't know where Perkins or the sergeant was and hoped she could get out on patrol before either one of them crossed her path. She didn't trust her actions because right then, she was so wound up, just a slight touch would surely spin her out of control.

The cell phone in her pocket vibrated, and she pulled it out. Paige had texted her asking if she was free. She clicked over to her recent calls and punched a button.

"Hello, Officer," Paige said when she answered.

"Hey yourself." Chris walked down the hall and stepped outside. Like it always was, the parking lot was full of police cars and officers coming and going, so she went around to the side of the building.

"Okay, what's wrong?"

Chris told her about the DV call.

"Fuck," Paige said. "That sergeant has always been an ass, but now he's a crooked cop, too?"

"Looks like it."

"What are you gonna do?"

"I'm waiting to see what Perkins writes in his report."

"Have you written yours?"

"I started it, but I'm all fucked up about this."

"I would be, too. Listen, don't let his tunnel vision or the sergeant's lies influence you. You didn't do anything wrong. If anything, you held back and handled the call the right way. Perkins didn't."

"You know, I used to think that all I had to do was walk that thin blue line. I believed that if I always followed the rules and stayed on the right side, I'd never have any problems. But now I feel like I've been slimed by a shitty situation, and all I can think about is that my actions are going to be questioned."

"What did you do after all that happened?"

Chris paused because she knew what Paige was asking. It didn't happen often, but Paige had witnessed times when stress would drive her to punishing amounts of alcohol, and it had been awful. "I got shitfaced."

"Oh, Chris. It's been more than three years since you've done that."

"I didn't break anything this time. I just…yelled a little."

"At who?"

Chris had pushed it out of her mind until just then. A massive ape-sized gathering of remorse crawled up her back and smothered her head. The stupid things she'd said still echoed in her ears. Her senseless behavior had fallen to an all-new low. "Sarah."

"You got drunk with Sarah?"

"No, I was by myself. Sarah just showed up."

"What did you say to her?"

"Nothing I remember as being horrible."

"Have you talked to her?"

"No. And I should, but I just want to get through my shift first."

"Well, no matter how this plays out with the DV call, you're in the right, and all you have to do is tell the truth."

"I wish it were that easy."

"I suppose if you and I wanted to stay away from politics in our areas of employment, we'd have to move to Ireland and sign up as sheepherders."

"No, thanks. You suck at camping under the stars."

"No, I don't!"

"Do I need to remind you about the trip to Lake Tahoe?"

"I don't like peeing anywhere that a stick could get shoved up my ass when I bend down."

"Driving all the way to the casinos every time you had to go to the bathroom isn't true camping behavior."

"Yeah, but I made great campfire breakfasts, didn't I?"

"That you did."

"Listen, Chris, you're a good cop. Hold your head high like you always do."

"I'll try."

"Did that help?"

Chris loved her best friend. "No."

❖

Sarah had just finished watching the eleven o'clock news and was turning off the television to go to bed when her doorbell rang. Cautiously, she looked through the peephole and saw Chris.

They hadn't spoken that day so she was glad Chris had thought to come by.

She opened the door to the same sight as the night before. Chris teetered on her step, and her expression, drawn limp from the numbing effect of whatever alcohol she'd consumed, was also slightly vacant.

"Hi," Chris said.

"Hello."

"Oh…" Chris wobbled as if just the raising of her eyebrows had thrown her equilibrium off. "You're not happy to see me."

"I'm not happy to see you drunk."

"Well, that's just great."

"Lower your voice, please."

"I just wanted to see you."

"And you got in your car and drove here?"

"Of course I…I'm fine, all right?"

"No, you're not."

"Okay, I'm going."

Sarah took her arm just as Chris tried to turn around, and they both stumbled off the step.

"Stop, Chris. You're not getting back in your car."

Chris jerked her arm away. "I can fucking drive."

Taking out her phone, Sarah said, "I'm calling a taxi. You can leave your car here."

"Oh. I'm being sent to my room, huh? I can't even come in?"

She spoke to a dispatch operator and gave her the address while Chris fumed and swore. "Chris," she said when she hung up, "this is not the way to handle things."

"This is a fine way to handle things."

"Really?"

"You know me, Sarah. I'm a good person…"

"It doesn't have anything to do with that. You know I hate it when people drink to excess. I've had too many horrible nights dealing with my parents to be happy about your binges."

"I'm not your parent. I don't drink every day, Sarah."

"It only takes one time to crash your car."

"You're mad, and I get it."

No, she doesn't, Sarah thought. It disappointed and scared her that Chris drank like this. Once in a while was just as bad as a hundred times, because each time, along with the rancid smell of booze came the horrible, lost feelings from childhood. Standing there, with Chris sloshed and weaving right in front of her, made Sarah suddenly feel small again, as if she didn't matter. She re-experienced the pain of knowing that, just as in her childhood, the booze seemed more important than she was.

Chris kept talking about problems and handling things, but it sounded like she was almost talking to herself. Sarah studied her as she rambled on. A drunk person's face hung on their skull in a certain way, as if the stitching in their muscles had just begun to fray and come apart. She'd seen it so many times before and hated it even more now.

"And I know who you are," Chris said. "I see who you are and—"

"That's the thing, Chris." Sarah's calm had imploded. "You don't see who I am. I don't think anyone can, really." Something deep and disturbing was surfacing, and she raised her voice because she couldn't stop the words from exploding out of the recesses of her mind.

"What does that mean?"

"You're saying that you know who I am, but Chris, no one does. And that's because I don't know who the fuck I am. All I do know is that I'm a faceless person whose only definitive belief is that what I can't quite remember is the thing I can't forget." She stopped talking and gritted her teeth until it hurt. This was no time to get into a conversation about her life. It wasn't the focus of the issue of Chris's drinking. "We can talk about this later, Chris."

"I think I'm getting the blow-off now." Chris's head swayed as she frowned. "Do you know how hard it is to toe the line?"

"I know how easy it is to pour a drink and pretend to forget. I watched my parents do that my whole life."

Chris held up two fingers as if pinching something that was an inch thick. "I have to live in this much space. All the time. You step out of it and you're fucked. If I make a mistake during an arrest, or send Abel to bite when I shouldn't, or even forget to Mirandize someone, I'm up shit creek. I can't screw up. Because if I do, I'm no better than the bad guys. Don't you see? There's no room for errors."

"I think those are your father's words, not yours."

Chris blinked as if Sarah had just sprayed her with water. "There's no other way to be."

"Yes, there is, Chris. There's the spirit of the law instead of the letter of the law. It's discretionary decision making. You can say *fuck it* to following strict convention and draw your own lines."

"I wouldn't have the career I have and the stability I have if it wasn't for living within the lines."

"At what price?"

"What price?! I'm not homeless, I have a roof over my head, and I have a pension for retirement. There's always a price for being responsible. I don't come from wealthy parents, Sarah. I need to work."

"I understand that, but there's a lot of space between right and wrong."

"That's a whole lot of bullshit."

Sarah ignored her snipe. "There's more to life than the extremes, Chris. You can't just cram everyone and everything into either all good or all bad. Including yourself. It doesn't work that way."

"It does in my job. There's no room for a mushy, vague middle ground. A criminal might be an okay person most of the time, but if he commits a crime, there's no gray area to muck around in. He gets arrested. That's my job."

"I'm not talking about your job. I'm talking about us."

"Am I supposed to change who I am when I'm off the clock? I was raised to live a certain way, and it can't just stop when I park my squad car."

"You're not understanding me, Chris."

"What am I not understanding?"

"If things go exactly by your rules, you're great. But if they don't, you're a bad person who grabs a bottle and punishes herself. It's like your job puts you in the impossible position of having to be perfect. And if you step just a little out of line, you're a piece of shit."

"That's the way it's always been."

"That's no excuse, Chris."

"That's easy for you to say. I *have* to work. And I risk my life for my paycheck. What do you do, walk to the mailbox?"

Even through her well-oiled brain, Chris obviously knew what she'd said had hurt Sarah. And it had. Terribly.

"I'm sorry, Sarah—"

"Just stop." The one woman who she thought would never use such sharp words had stabbed Sarah's heart. She held up her hand as if she could shield herself from any more. "You've had enough to drink and you've said enough."

A taxi pulled up and flashed its lights.

"There's your ride." Sarah didn't trust her voice to long sentences. Hot tears were building quickly.

"I'm sorry, Sarah. I really am."

"Go home, Chris."

"Please let me stay."

"Go. Now." She turned and went back into the house. Chris was still talking as she closed the door and locked it. She needed to get to her room before she broke down but only made it to the hallway, where she slid to the carpet and crumpled into a ball of despair.

CHAPTER THIRTEEN

Chris had two hours left in her shift when she got a call to assist two of her partners at a bar in Hollywood. They were arresting a female for a warrant and needed Chris to search her.

It had been a crap-filled day. Call after call was filled with stupid people dealing drugs and beating their spouses. She'd had it with the dregs of society. The hot sun that afternoon had done nothing but poke her repeatedly, like the schoolyard brat that you weren't allowed to smack. The nausea from drinking the night before, too many cups of acidic coffee, and no lunch had disintegrated whatever stomach lining she had left, and her guts surged every time she turned a corner.

She'd been a complete ass to Sarah. Why had she gone over there anyway? She'd clearly been too drunk to drive, and stupidly, she had anyway. That was a huge fuck-up on her part. She'd never gotten into a car during one of her "events." She was angry with herself for being so reckless and irresponsible.

But she was completely disgusted by what she'd said to Sarah. She'd basically called her a jobless nobody. She winced at the memory of Sarah's face and suddenly felt like she was going to puke again.

How could she have been so cruel? Her own problems were so stuck up her ass that she had to lash out at a woman she was... what? Falling in love with?

She stopped at a light and glared at the crossing traffic ambling by so carefree and happy. A dark, broiling cloud of a notion to pull those people over just to ruin their day made her even more appalled at herself.

Was she really falling in love? She'd let her guard down with Jen, and that had led to a lot of pain. She remembered a conversation she'd had with Paige. It had been about her ex.

"Jen used to rub my back when I came home. I miss that."
"Do you miss her?"
"No. I just miss the caretaking. Our relationship never really went anywhere, you know? And there was a reason I never asked her to move in. It just didn't feel right. Except for the back rubs."

She'd supported Jen financially and then got stomped on. Was she afraid she'd end up taking care of Sarah as well?

That was such an idiotic notion. Hell, Sarah came from money and didn't need her for anything like that.

So what the hell had made her say those things to her?

Chris rolled up to the bar where Billings and Davidson were standing outside with a short, rather large Hispanic woman.

"What's up?" she said when Billings stepped over to her.

"Ran her. She's got a warrant and I think she's holding."

"Meth?"

"What else? We cuffed her but wanted you to search her."

Chris walked back to where Davidson was watching the woman and noticed she was standing right at the bar entrance. A few men were on the other side of the doorway, a little too close for safety, so she said, "Step over here so we can talk."

The woman became tense and scrunched her face up. She was drunk, and it was obvious that alcohol brought out the belligerence in her. She took a few steps away, but not enough for Chris's liking. She motioned to Billings and Davidson to stand in front of the door and turned back to the woman. "What's your name?"

"Madonna." Spittle came out of her mouth.

Nice. "What's your name?"

"Lady Gaga."

With the last scrap of politeness she could muster, she said, "Okay. I'm going to search you and then we can talk some more."

Chris reached for her cuffed hands to secure her, and as soon as she did, the woman tried to jerk away. One foot came back and kicked Chris in the shin. Chris grabbed her hair and forced her to the ground. As they hit the pavement, Chris felt a sharp pain across her kneecap and quickly rolled her body around so she had her full weight on the suspect.

The woman kept struggling, so Chris wrenched the woman's arms backward and up into a very unnatural position, which would hurt enough to get her attention.

"Stop resisting," Chris yelled. Finally she complied and Chris pushed herself off the woman. She picked her up and took her to the car, while Billings and Davidson dissuaded the crowd at the door from joining them outside.

"Do you have anything illegal on you?"

"Bitch, no."

Chris patted her down, and the typical aroma of sweat and too much perfume stung her nose. She didn't find anything in her pants pockets.

There was, however, a slight bulge in her front shirt pocket, so Chris reached in and pulled out a small piece of wrapped plastic that contained about a half gram of meth.

"I'm going to ask you again. Do you have anything illegal on you?"

"Fuck you, you cunt."

Chris actually heard her brain snap. It was a split-second noise, like a fresh carrot being broken in half.

"Fuck me?" Chris screamed. "No, fuck you, you bitch! You fight with me and cause me to rip my pants, and then you call *me* a cunt?"

Davidson looked at her and hastily shook his head.

The woman started to tell her to fuck off, and Chris thwacked her on the forehead with her fingertips. "Shut up."

She spun the woman around and rifled through her remaining pockets, finding a few condoms, which she immediately dropped on the ground, and two more small baggies of meth.

When Chris was satisfied that she had nothing else hidden on her, she took her arm and led her over to Billings and Davidson.

She handed them the contraband and said, "This little princess is all yours."

Billings dropped his chin and looked at her through his eyebrows. "You good?"

"Yeah. Just peachy."

❖

Chris drove away and found a church parking lot that was as empty as a golf course on Mother's Day. She didn't want anyone to bother her while she got herself together.

It was stupid to go off on that woman. How many drunks and drug dealers did she deal with nightly? How often had she been called the C-word or been told to fuck off? Probably as regularly as a convenience-store clerk rings up a six-pack of beer. It was a standard transaction for her, but she'd let that woman get under her skin.

You idiot, she said to herself, and hit her steering wheel.

Abel whined from the back of the car.

You're losing it and you need to get your shit together.

She looked at her phone. No messages from Sarah. She hadn't called either, because she'd been ashamed, and nothing about the crap-hole day had allowed her a moment of respite to think of something halfway decent to say to her.

She put her head back against the headrest and closed her eyes. *Just calm down for a second. Think about how you feel about her.*

Flashes of her words to Sarah and even that meth-toting woman poked at her, provoking her relentlessly, like bratty kids taunting a feeble babysitter.

Fuck me? No, fuck you!

Easy for you to say. I risk my life for my paycheck. What do you do, walk to the mailbox?

And you call me a cunt?

She was too pissed at herself to clear her head.

"Aagghhh," she yelled and threw the car door open. Abel barked, ready to jump into whatever confrontation had his alpha so agitated.

She paced the parking lot, breathing in deeply and expelling the air like a Spanish bull facing a smug matador. Her heart pounded and her jaw cramped from clenching her teeth. She was angry, looking for something, anything, to lash out at. She picked up a stick and hurled it toward a row of trees.

Nothing was going right. She wished she could just log out of her computer, take Abel home, and crawl into bed. She found a number of other sticks and larger branches and sent them toward the trees as well.

After some time, her feet grew heavy and she slowed her pace, as if something had gouged her fuel tank and she was rapidly running out of gas. She stopped and felt her body swaying, vulnerable to anything stronger than a gust of wind. She dropped to a squat and covered her head with her arms.

"Today went south because of the way you acted last night," Chris muttered. "Sarah's right about your Achilles's heel. Every time you go on a binge, you aim an arrow right at the back of your ankle and shoot to maim."

She looked up at the sky. It was dark, but she could no

longer see a trace of soot or ashes from the recent blazes. Like the current fire season in Los Angeles, things had flared up between them, but now they needed to get back to normal.

"You love her," she said as she stood slowly. "You fucked up and you need to make it right."

She sat back down in the car, feeling alone and miserable. Abel had quieted down, leaving just the chatter over the police radio reverberating around the squad car. There was a lot of activity that afternoon, more than usual. She could tune a lot of it out because cops trained their ears to pick up the transmission intended for them. She supposed it was a lot like a mother who could pick out her children's voices in a playground full of kids. The crackly dialogues from license-plate runs to robberies and assaults and suspect descriptions were just buzzes and hums until she was called. Then, every detail was recorded in her memory way before she was able to jot it down on a pad of paper.

Sure enough, her ears suddenly tuned in to the varied exchanges.

"Frank K9, Frank one-fifty-six."

Her shift lieutenant was calling out her designator.

"Frank K9, go ahead."

"I need you to hold over for six hours."

The K9 handler for the next shift must have called in sick. She needed to see Sarah and now she couldn't. At least not right away. This was going to be a long, tedious night.

"Copy that, sir.

"Fuck." She glanced down to make sure she was off the air.

On the heels of that transmission, a burglary call came in, and within a few minutes, the responding officers called her to assist them in a search. As she headed toward the address, she called Sarah. If she could at least start a conversation over the phone, maybe it would ease things until she could see her.

Sarah's voice mail picked up, but Chris hung up before leaving an answer. She wasn't really ready to leave a message. Then again, she didn't even know exactly what she wanted to say if Sarah answered. All she knew was that if she heard her voice, she'd find the courage to talk.

Chris pulled up to an adult clothing store on La Cienega. The responding officers told her they believed the suspect was still inside. The front window was smashed and the alarm still screamed its distress.

She got Abel out, hooked up his leash, and took him to the broken front window. Abel barked a few times, ready for work.

A few lights were on inside the store, and Chris could see displays of clothing, mostly lingerie, on mannequins and on circular racks. Areas of the store had been ransacked, and a pile of clothing and other items lay in the middle of the store. Close by, someone had toppled a mannequin over.

A mass of small, shiny pebbles lying on the ground just inside the store told her the window was made of safety glass, which was good. With her nightstick, she cleared the remaining glass away from the bottom sill to minimize the chance of Abel sustaining foot cuts.

Abel was straining on his leash, barking hysterically when she made her announcement.

"Los Angeles Police K9. Come out with your hands up, or I'll send my dog in and he will bite you."

Nobody moved inside.

She repeated her announcement, louder this time, to be heard over the alarm.

"Los Angeles Police K9. If you're hiding in there, you're gonna get bit."

Abel jumped and pulled at the leash, barking constantly now.

With no response, Chris unhooked Abel and he dove through the window. Chris hurriedly jumped in right behind him.

Abel went right for a downed mannequin that lay on the floor. Dogs weren't perfect and sometimes the frenzy of the moment would make them bypass their sense of smell and go after anything that looked human.

Chris began to call Abel off when the mannequin started to scream.

In the few seconds it took for the two officers to cuff the man and for her to command Abel to release his bite, she could tell that the suspect had taken off his clothes and put on a short skirt and halter top. He obviously thought it would be a good plan to lie down on the ground and pretend to be a mannequin that had fallen over.

Chris spared the man the same laughter that the other officers now showered upon him, but it was a pretty funny sight.

Back in her car, she made notes that would be part of the bite report required of each incident. Every sentence or two, she stopped, feeling as if a vacuum whose label read REMORSE, THE BEST BRAND IN GUILT SUCKING had drawn out her energy.

She'd hurt Sarah and needed so desperately to see her. Her drunkenness and callousness had screwed everything up. Their relationship had been so exciting and enjoyable, flowing as gently as a slow river in summer. Now, she was standing alone in the middle of a torrent of white water. She couldn't, and wouldn't, try to swim away from the strong current of regret that crashed unforgivingly against her. She would withstand anything, especially in penance of her own dreadful mistakes, if it would help fix things with Sarah.

She tried to call Sarah but hung up when her voice mail clicked on again. She stared at the glowing face of the phone, displaying a picture of Abel she'd taken when he was first assigned to her. She wished she could go back to the first day she met Sarah. And if she couldn't do that, she'd just ask to go back a couple of days to change the way she'd behaved.

She clicked over to messages and typed.

Sarah, I didn't thank you for helping me when I was sick. Actually, drunk. And I want to tell you how I regret being so horribly wretched to you last night when I was drunk yet again. Two hugely stupid mistakes. And the third mistake, worst of all, is that I was an idiot and was callous to you. I am asking for the opportunity to apologize in person.

She reread the text. It was a start, she supposed. She hit send and wished she could be transported to Sarah as quickly as the message whooshed to her.

❖

As she pulled into her garage, Chris hit a few keystrokes on her dash-mounted computer to sign off of her shift and turned off the car's engine. The nightly routine was more like a ritual for Abel and her. She let him out and he sat in front of her, fidgeting excitedly because he never wasn't excited. She took his vest off and his tail wagged eagerly. His ears were alert and his eyes focused on nothing else but her.

"Did you do well today, Abel?" she said quietly.

His tail wagged even harder.

"Are you the best partner ever?"

Out of habit, his body shook with anticipation.

She paused, watching him hang on her every movement and word, and said, "Good boy!"

He leaped up and she caught him as he hit her full force in the chest. He slobbered all over her face, and she was, as always, filled with pride and love as she let him back down.

He waited for her at the garage side door, ran into the backyard when she said it was okay, and peed when she told him to take a break. He then let himself into his kennel. She fed him, locked the door, and as she went inside, she checked her phone. She didn't have any calls or texts from Sarah.

She threw her keys on the counter, but they slid off and landed on the floor. She walked by them and stopped, backtracked, and picked them up.

As she placed them on the counter, she said, "Nice, Bergstrom. The floor is bad. The counter is good. You couldn't just leave them there because that would be *bad*." She snatched up her keys again and cocked her arm back to launch them at the wall.

Her frustration and disappointment over the way she'd treated Sarah had been building since that night. A foul burst of anger exploded inside her but evaporated just as suddenly, and the withdrawal wrenched her gut. As if someone had suddenly knocked the wind out of her, her knees buckled and she reached out to lean on the counter.

Her cell phone rang and she fumbled through her pocket to get it. Sarah, she thought, thank God.

"Bergstrom." It was Sergeant Shaffer.

"What the hell happened at the bar call with Davidson and Billings?"

"What do you mean?"

"You mouthed off to that suspect."

"She assaulted me."

"What am I supposed to do when the suspect lodges a formal complaint?"

"I guess you'll have to take that complaint."

"Cut the shit. I'm thinking of writing you up for it."

"Yes, sir." She closed her eyes and mouthed the F-word.

CHAPTER FOURTEEN

At three o'clock in the morning, Chris was still in her uniform pants and undershirt. She hadn't showered, which wasn't a good thing after pulling overtime on a sixteen-hour shift. But she didn't really care.

She hadn't done anything but sit outside and swirl in a toilet bowl of her own bullshit. A thousand re-creations of her last conversation with Sarah weren't going to change things. No matter what she could have, or should have, said mattered as little as hitting the brakes after your car has gone over a cliff.

She'd fucked up royally, all within one twenty-four-hour period.

How had things changed so drastically? She and Sarah had been doing well and really getting to know each other. Sure, they had personality differences, but the whole opposites-attract notion seemed to work with other people.

It did with Paige and Avalon. Those two were from different worlds. Sure, Paige worked in the same entertainment industry as Avalon, but she was a photographer and wrote coffee-table books, whereas Avalon was a famous actress. Paige was grounded and Avalon was a bit wild.

They had a lot of ups and downs, but they worked them out.

But had Sarah written her off? Was she fuming, gathering

a maelstrom of words to throw back at her? That would be fine, Chris thought. She deserved it. She'd take anything that would allow her to hear Sarah's voice again.

But her phone had remained unsympathetically silent.

She typed another message to Sarah.

I can't sleep. I don't know where you are. I'm sitting on my front porch and it's foggy, damp, and eerily quiet. I can hear water drip off the roof of another house. A coyote just yapped for a minute somewhere just north of me. I heard a bunny scurry across a neighbor's yard three houses down. I hear a frog croak every so often down the street. No birds. I'll bet they're roosting somewhere, tucked in their wings for the night. It's like my senses are hypersensitive right now as I sit here. It's a strange feeling.

And I want to yell as loud as possible. To scream to the world how sorry I am that I hurt you. How I regret that while you were trying to help me and explain things to me, I just wouldn't listen. I want to yell until it breaks through the fog so you can get my message.

❖

It was past four in the morning when Chris finally went to bed. She closed her eyes, telling herself to fall asleep, which was as successful as demanding a tree to drop its leaves. At some point she must have drifted off, but within two hours, the sun was up, poking at her eyelids.

Before she was even fully awake, Chris reached for her phone and felt the lead weight in her heart sink to the bottom of a pool of gloom. Still no calls or texts from Sarah.

Her eyes hurt and a headache was prying at her skull, attempting to gain access and beat the shit out of her brain. Sitting up didn't help much, so she got up and swallowed some aspirin.

Wandering around the house, she went into the living room

and stood behind the couch. After a minute, she wondered why the hell she was staring at the magazines on the coffee table. She plodded into the kitchen and opened the refrigerator. Again, she stared at nothing but finally grabbed a Diet Coke just so she'd avoid getting pissed that she was caught in an aimless circle.

She could think of absolutely nothing positive to do. Making breakfast didn't appeal to her, and the thought of doing laundry sucked. She had the morning off, to do anything she wanted, but the empty span of time seemed like a prison sentence because she couldn't talk to the one person she needed to reach.

She certainly wasn't going to stalk Sarah or call her every ten minutes. The ball was not only *not* in her court; it had been picked up and taken home.

She went back to her bedroom and grabbed her cell phone. She needed a friendly voice.

"Good morning, sunshine." Paige sounded like she'd been up for hours.

"Why are you so chipper?"

"I'm seeing my girl tonight, the concept for my new book is coming along brilliantly, and it's Thursday."

"What's so special about Thursday?"

"You've forgotten."

What had she forgotten? "Geez, Paige…my head's not right. I'm sorry."

"I can't believe it dropped out of your head that we're going to the Dapper Cadaver."

"Oh, yeah. I remember now," Chris said as she sat up in bed, rubbing her eyes. Paige needed props to use in a book-cover photo shoot she was planning. The theme had something to do with Hollywood horror movies, and the Dapper Cadaver was a prop house and fabrication shop that made all sorts of corpses and guts and body parts for films and television shows. They'd talked about it a few times and picked a day to go. That all had occurred before her life changed at the blackberry bin of Whole

Foods Market. "You want me to go see fake versions of what I see every day during my regular work hours?"

"Yup," she said a little too cheerfully. "You're my consultant."

"All right, but I need to be back before this afternoon."

"Going in to work early?"

"No," she said. However, that wouldn't be a bad idea. "I just need to be busy."

"What's the matter?"

Chris got up to brush her teeth, which tasted like hairy bits of taffy. "I'll tell you when you pick me up."

❖

Even long after rush hour was over, Interstate 5, the freeway that began in Mexico and didn't stop until reaching into Canada, had its typical clog of cars going Lord knows where. The sun beat down on the windshield, and Chris slouched in the passenger's seat as though she were in math class, her worst subject.

"Tell me what this adventure is about?" Chris glared at the trucker who stared down at her from his big rig.

"I already told you, like four times, we're going to a horror shop full of gory prop body parts."

"Oh, yeah." Things weren't sticking in her head lately. Maybe it was only those things that had nothing to do with Sarah.

"And quit changing the subject." Paige moved over a lane just as she crossed under the Ventura Freeway in Glendale. "So, you left off where you said some horrible things to Sarah and then she left."

"I was drunk."

"That's bullshit. The alcohol didn't form the words you said to her. You did."

Chris rubbed her forehead. "I know." She elaborated on

more of the conversation she'd had with Sarah, feeling nauseous just retelling the awful facts.

"So then what?"

"I haven't heard from her. I worked a long shift yesterday and texted her a couple of times. I guess she doesn't want to talk to me."

"Would you want to talk to you?"

"This pleasant chitchat in which we're partaking isn't helping."

Paige rolled her eyes and began to merge over to the slow lane. "It's called tough love."

"I need to find her and apologize. I want to ask her, if it's not too late, if I can try again."

"You think it's actually over between you?"

"I don't know. I can't get ahold of her. The evidence seems to point to a fait accompli."

"You're getting all French on me. Have you been arresting baguette bakers?"

Chris thought a moment about the term and its finality. "You know when you fire a gun?"

"No. I never have."

"Theoretically. Jesus, Paige. When you fire a gun and it shoots through a window, what's the result?"

"A call to the maid to bring a broom?"

Chris snatched up Paige's coffee from the middle console.

"Hey!" Paige reached for it unsuccessfully. "Give that back."

"You're being a brat."

"Okay, okay. Give Paige mommy's little helper."

Chris handed it back to her. "You get a presumably irreversible outcome."

Paige took the Hollywood Way off-ramp and turned south. "Probably. But until you talk to her, it's still a presumption."

Her phone hadn't vibrated all morning, but Chris checked

it again anyway. She saw Paige watching her and pushed it back into her front pocket.

"Listen, Chris, it's not over until the corpulent lady sings."

Chris snorted.

"You're not going to give up, are you?"

"No." She was just currently petrified to confront Sarah. And that was pretty funny because her job consisted of nothing but confrontation. Except, at work, she was always on the straightforward side of conflict. All she had to do was observe and listen to the facts and then hook 'em up or let 'em go. This time, she was the perpetrator. And she was thoroughly ashamed.

But she was also sick of moping around in her own shit. She needed to find Sarah and hope to hell she'd listen.

"Then what are you going to do?"

"I'm going to get out of this funk and face the music from the corpulent lady. And then I'm going to go over to her place and throw pebbles at her window if I have to."

"That's right. And you'll be fine. Just tell her how you feel."

As they pulled in front of a very stark and nondescript building on San Fernando Road, Chris sat up straight. "That's a lot of telling, but I'm ready."

A green, coffin-shaped graphic on the face of the building read DAPPER CADAVER—CASUALTY SIMULATION. While the rest of the building blended in with the other perfectly square, gray cement industrial structures that lined the block, the only other indication that bizarre things awaited them inside was a small sign next to the door. It was simply a hand-painted image of an "open" casket. In its restrained simplicity, the place looked absolutely chilling.

A Metrolink train lumbered by, which was the only movement in the neighborhood. Maybe it was early, Chris thought. Or maybe the zombies hadn't woken up yet and decided to come on down for a parts replacement.

Chris and Paige got out of the car and walked up to the door.

"This is gonna be cool!" Paige said, and they went in.

The entryway was decorated with jars of what looked like closed-eyed little animals and deformed something-or-others all floating in formaldehyde. Surgical instruments lined the glass cases of the front desk. Anatomical charts, skeletons, and bizarre mermaid-like creatures completed the décor.

A strangely normal-looking woman directed them into the warehouse—which struck Chris as more like a museum than a store. Disfigured bodies, weapons, and morgue instruments lived in gruesome harmony with semi-fleshy bones, burnt body parts, a couple of mummies, and a myriad of torture devices.

Chris almost nodded to the man in her peripheral vision, but he wouldn't return the gesture as it was actually a decapitated guy in a floral shirt and beach shorts.

Chris leaned toward Paige. "You always take me to the nicest places."

They wandered past the funeral caskets and a gutted, naked man with his intestines sprawled along the floor. Chris was so engrossed in the grossness of the eviscerated rubber humans and animals that she didn't see Paige stop and bumped into her.

A mass of dismembered, cut-up, and burnt corpses was propped up against a display wall of neatly arranged body parts that would make Hannibal Lecter swoon.

"This is exactly what I need."

"That's good to know," Chris said as she surveyed the amazing array of choice parts. "Remind me not to have any more sleepovers at your place."

Paige smacked her on the arm. "Admit it, this place is so creepy, it's a hoot!"

All Chris knew was that if she had to take Abel in here to conduct a search at night, she'd hope to hell her flashlight wouldn't crap out on her.

Paige picked up items like they were shoes at Payless

ShoeSource, except these styles had names like gory Jack half arm, bloody meat spine, human-torso skin, eye with optic nerve, and serial-killer scraps.

Chris picked up a piece called half-eaten arm. "Maybe I should give this to Abel to chew on when we interrogate suspected drug dealers."

Paige grabbed it from her. "Ooooh, this would be good, too."

"So what are you envisioning exactly?"

Paige's eyes were as wide and excited as a sugared-up kid at a slumber party. "I want to create a horror scene and have film equipment around it. Maybe a motion-picture camera with a bloody torso hanging over it, or a movie clapboard that's severing an arm."

"Okay, that's gruesome for a book cover."

"It'll be done so that it's obviously not real. That's the slant of the book. I'm photographing the behind-the-scenes of special horror effects and their applications on the set. I've already gotten shots of actors playing with things just like this."

"Well, I have to admit, this stuff looks pretty real." She marveled at the artistry in the production of the pieces. Obviously people were used to cast the body parts, and then someone pulled parts from a mold and painted them, but the level of detail was surprisingly believable. She got a kick out of watching Paige pore over her choices, holding up one gory thing and comparing it to another.

After a while, Paige picked out about five items and happily carried them to the front desk while Chris hung back and stared a mangled corpse straight in its only eye.

"Come on," Paige called when she'd finished making her purchase. "Let's go back to my place and lay all this out on the table!"

Chris nodded to the woman and then opened the door for Paige. "You play house with your new friends, and I'll go home and not think about eating a steak for a while."

❖

Uniformed and ready for work, Chris loaded Abel in the back of her squad car and drove over to Sarah's house. She had more than a half hour before she had to log in for her shift and hoped she would talk to her.

Frazzled nerves danced at the ends of her arms, making her hands shake. What would she say to Sarah? How should the conversation start?

First of all, Sarah, I am so sorry...
Sarah, please give me a minute to tell you...
Here's the thing, I was an asshole.

Would Sarah slam the door in her face?

She turned on to Holly Oak Drive and wound her way up to Sarah's house. There was no car in the driveway, but that didn't mean her car wasn't in the garage. Chris parked on the street and hushed Abel when he barked, telling her that he wanted to come with her.

As she approached the front door, she saw only one light on inside the house. She rang the doorbell, unnerved by the awkward shaking of her legs. Listening for footsteps, she didn't hear any. No radio or television noise either. She rang again and strained to hear any signs of Sarah approaching the door. Her radio suddenly squawked and she abruptly sucked in her breath.

"Shit," she said as she turned the volume down.

She waited a minute or two longer and walked back down to the driveway. She checked both sides of the house and found nothing.

Abel barked again when she climbed back into her car.

"Nobody home, boy." She looked toward the front windows, hoping for movement from the drapes and then for Sarah's face to peek out, see her, and smile that sexy smile of hers. She laughed out loud. "Jesus, Bergstrom, this isn't a movie."

Chris's spirit, dampened by the disappointment, slumped inside her chest as she logged in to the computer and began prioritizing the calls that were waiting for her.

❖

At half past seven p.m., Chris pulled up to a coffee stand on Santa Monica Boulevard. The diminutive shack was on the corner of a strip-mall parking lot. It was a run-down, tired-looking building whose paint constantly peeled, showing more scrapings of color than a peacock who'd just lost a fight. The place served as a local hangout for prostitutes. It was also a good place for a reliable cup of joe and even more reliable information.

"Officer Bergy." A tall woman in blue hot pants and a red halter-top sashayed up to her as Chris exited the car. Her wig was made up into a chocolate-sundae-looking bouffant that took only partial attention away from the substantial volume of costume jewelry hanging from her arms and the overbearing aroma of perfume that evoked a mix of Juicy Fruit gum and Play-Doh.

"Foxy Turf," Chris said. She was one of her best informants. "How's my favorite Girl Scout?"

"Oh, darlin', that was weeks ago."

"Well, don't let me catch you trying to get a date in that get-up again. I almost hooked you up and took you to Child Protective Services."

Foxy's mouth opened to a wide smile that revealed an orifice of hit-or-miss teeth. "Ha! You funny. But that get-up is worth at least twenny dollas mo than normal."

"The old men like that, huh?"

"Does the tin man have a metal cock, honey?"

Chris pondered a moment. "Well, you've got a real good point there."

"You gonna buy me a coffee tonight, Officer Bergy?"

Chris felt her phone vibrate. She quickly reached into her

shirt pocket, pulled out a five-dollar bill, and handed it to her. "Gotta take this call."

She walked back to her car and almost dropped her phone trying to answer it.

"Hello?"

"Chris. What the hell's going on?"

It was her father. And though she knew exactly why he was calling, she said, "What do you mean?"

"I was informed that you got out of line with a suspect."

She stopped next to her car. "Father, I was—"

"You were what? What excuse do you have? That's not how Bergstroms handle calls, Chris. What were you thinking?"

I'm thinking this is the last fucking thing I need right now. "You never lost it with some idiot?"

"Not in the way you did. And I'm also aware of your lack of judgment in failing to deploy your K9."

She tensed as a flash of hot anger raced up her body. She now knew who had called him. What a fucking asshole. "I'm not even going to have this conversation with you, Father. If Shaffer had actually been there, he would have seen that I made the correct decision."

"Are you calling him a liar?"

Chris almost doubled over from the sharp pain of those words. Her own father wouldn't even give her the benefit of the doubt. She wanted to wail as loud as she could. She wanted to kick the shit out of the door. But she wouldn't allow him to hear the agony in her voice. "I'm getting a call. I have to go."

"Don't disappoint me again, Chris."

She ended the call and leaned into her car, transported back to when she was five years old and he was telling her that good little girls don't whistle. And then to the time when she was ten and he berated her for leaving a shirt on the floor. And then to the million other times she strayed off the straight and narrow, until she learned how to walk on the edge of a razor. And even after she'd beaten herself into his impossible mold, she still wasn't good enough.

❖

Chris parked at the apex of the circular driveway. Bel Air was out of her area, but she had to make the trip. Since it was a little before eight, they might be having dinner, but if she waited until after her shift, it would be close to ten thirty at night, when a ring at the doorbell would not be as well received.

Mrs. Pullman answered the door and didn't recognize her. "Oh, my. What's wrong, Officer?"

"I'm Chris, Mrs. Pullman. Sarah's girlfriend. From Father's Day."

"Is something wrong?"

"Not really," Chris said, glancing down at her uniform. "I'm on duty and this was the best time for me to come by. I was hoping you'd talked with her recently."

Mrs. Pullman paused in the way a suspect did when asked of their recent whereabouts. "I haven't. But that's not unusual."

"Do you know where she might be?"

"If she's not at home or at the refuge, then, no."

Mrs. Pullman didn't seem to be lying. Sarah had said that she wasn't a fixture at the parental house anymore. So why did Mrs. Pullman delay for a moment before she answered?

"I haven't seen Sarah for a number of days, and I'm worried about her."

Chris almost cringed when Mrs. Pullman's face turned into the frozen smile of a scarecrow. Something behind her expression gave Chris the willies. "Sarah doesn't inform me of her excursions. And she's an adult now."

What the fuck did "excursions" mean? Chris pulled out a card and handed it to her. "If you do see her, would you have her call me, please?"

Again, she hesitated. "I will."

Chris had heard that neighborly response many times before. It was meant to convey a simultaneous impression of both a confidence and innocence.

But of what?

Chris got back in her car wondering, *now what am I going to do?* The waiting was excruciating. She hadn't seen Sarah since last Tuesday, and her anxiety had grown from a trickle to a deluge.

With each hour that passed, bad things had to be developing. At worst, Sarah was hurt somewhere. That notion frightened her. Without any way to reach her, Chris was impotent. At best, Sarah was okay and pissed at her, but without being able to talk, Chris imagined the last words she'd spat at her had to be growing more and more vile in Sarah's mind. The longer they were apart, the worse things would get. The true comprehension of that vile behavior weighed her down as heavily as a solid-oak oxen bow.

Maybe Sarah had already written her off. That was a definite possibility, but Chris had to see her, face-to-face, to know for sure.

And the other reason she had to see her, the foremost motivation that drove her, was that she did love her. The heaviness in her chest was her heart swelling with desire.

She fingered her radio call button, contemplating an act that was prohibited. Officers weren't supposed to commit unlawful exploits under color of authority. She'd never crossed that line. Residing ardently on the north side of those principles had been an easy practice and a steadfast tradition.

But the line had recently begun to blur, the significance becoming as distorted as a child's sidewalk chalk drawing after a rainstorm. Desire was not a simple emotion. It lived on both sides of the line. Its hold on her felt both right and wrong and irrepressibly forceful. Chris couldn't control her aching for Sarah any more than she could hold back from cursing that drunken, swearing woman.

No longer was the world so black and white. The

circumstances between Sarah and her made up the complicated part, but the feelings and emotions were raw and simple. Sarah was gone and she had to find her.

All she had to do was push the button.

Push the button.

Finally, she keyed her radio.

"Frank K9, are you clear to run a plate?"

"Go ahead."

The speaker sounded like Lee, one of their oldest and best dispatchers.

She remembered her first date with Sarah, up in Laurel Canyon, when she had seen Sarah's Tesla during her endearing ruse to get a kiss. "Five-Robert-Tom-Adam-One-Two-Seven."

Throughout the five or so seconds of dead air, sweat filtered through her skin and left a moist spot above her lip.

"Negative 29, it's a current 2014 Tesla," Lee said. It wasn't stolen. "10-28," she said, "is current to a last of Pullman, first of Sarah, out of Hollywood."

"Copy, thank you."

A rush of contrition washed through her. And to make it worse, she'd gotten nothing useful from her wrongful request. What was she thinking, that she'd hear from the dispatcher that the car was registered to a secret address where Sarah was hiding out or that it was currently sitting at a McDonald's in West Hollywood?

Yes, she rationalized, if it were stolen, she would have cause to conduct an official search, but even then, she'd have no legitimate reason to have called it in.

She'd simply reached out, to anything that was connected to Sarah, to be as close as possible.

"Frank K9, clear to respond to past call?"

"Frank K9, clear."

"Are you available to assist unit Three-Lincoln-Nine with a vehicle search?"

"Affirmative. En route."

The address, including a cross street, appeared on her computer screen.

As she turned her car around toward the location, the cop in her wondered how else she could find connections to Sarah.

She turned north and Abel whined, knowing why she increased her speed.

There was one way. But she'd have to go back to Sarah's.

CHAPTER FIFTEEN

Thirty minutes after her shift was over, Chris had changed into jeans and a dark-green T-shirt, jumped into her civilian car, and was pulling up to Sarah's street. A few cars were still driving around her neighborhood at half past ten, and Chris checked each one in case it was Sarah's.

She pulled up to the house and got out. The driveway was still empty and the house looked just as unoccupied as it did earlier. She walked up to the front door and rang the bell again, just in case. When no one answered, she peered through the front window and waited until her eyes adjusted to the unlit room. She wasn't expecting to find out much. Sure enough, nothing looked out of place or disturbed in a way that would indicate a struggle. Pillows sat neatly on the couch and a darkened lamp sat on a side table. Light drifted in from the hallway, giving few details of anything else.

She turned away and paused. What had been on the side table, just under the lamp? She pulled a small flashlight from her pocket and shined it through the window.

It was Sarah's cell phone. Chris called the number and watched as it came to life, its LED light casting a bluish glow on the underside of the lamp's shade.

As Sarah's voice mail came on, Chris hung up and turned off the flashlight. She was gone and didn't have her cell. Why?

She walked off the porch and to the right side of the house. Large bushes sealed the house to the dividing wall, so she went over to the other side. There she found a pathway, so she followed it. The gate she encountered was wooden, about six feet high, with a white coat of paint. She tried the handle but it wouldn't open, so she reached over the top and was able to unfasten the latch.

She went around the perimeter of Sarah's house, shining a flashlight in every window. Chris wanted to find her but was fearful she'd see her slumped over a chair or motionless on the floor. Each room she checked was empty. She stopped at Sarah's bedroom and looked in. Her bed was made and some clothes were folded on her dresser, but that was it. She just wasn't there.

Chris made her way back to the side gate and stopped at a trash can and a recycling bin. She retrieved her flashlight again, held it in her mouth, and removed the trash can lid.

It was less than one-quarter full of old food, a dead plant, some broken glass, and some juice and milk cartons. Sarah was good at separating her non-recyclables.

Chris closed the lid and opened the recycling bin. In it were the usual bottles and cans, and as quietly as she could, Chris moved them aside to pull out the items of paper—mostly unopened envelopes of what looked like junk mail. She separated those from the rest of the paper and put them back into the can.

She then inspected what she had left—a couple of notes that looked like self-reminders and grocery lists that she divided from the rest and put at the bottom of her stack. Various credit-card receipts were left.

The grocery receipts joined the junk mail, and she read through the rest as quickly as she could. She stopped when she got to the last one.

"Fuck," she whispered. She had no idea what might help

her, but whatever it was, it wasn't here. What a stupid chance she was taking going through Sarah's trash like a crazy person.

She flipped through each one again, shaking her head in frustration and muttering, "Ralph's grocery. The dry cleaners. An ATM receipt. Shell gas station. A restaurant…"

The signature caught her eye. It wasn't like the rest and she looked closer. The printed name under the signature was Natalie Crowden.

She was Sarah's best friend, the one she went to China with, the cricket-fighting girl. Even the receipt was an example of Sarah's exciting spirit. The name of the place was Nyala Ethiopian Cuisine. Chris had no idea there even was an African restaurant in Los Angeles.

She thought about Sarah's adventurous life, envying her daring nature. Sarah wasn't afraid to try new things or make mistakes. She lived in refreshing contrast to Chris's stiffness, her obsession with procedure and rules. Sarah did live in the grays, the places where Chris would never venture, but Sarah's experiences weren't that extreme, really. It wasn't like she lived a life of petty crime. She was just brave enough to step out of her own way.

In retrospect, Chris had never done that. And maybe it was time she did.

As she looked down at the receipt, reading that they'd ordered eccentric things called Yabesha Gommen, Yawaze Tibs, and Yebere Wet, it became apparent that if Chris wanted to stay within the strict world of black and white, she'd never get any closer to Sarah.

She turned the receipt over and squinted at the pen scratches. It looked like the private part of a woman, but it also looked like some kind of diagram.

She stuffed the receipt in her pocket, returned the rest of the paper items to the recycle bin, and walked out the gate.

❖

The only Natalie Crowden that came up on the Internet was a Facebook account. Luckily, Natalie had set her viewing preferences to public and Chris searched her photo albums. It didn't take long to find pictures of her with Sarah, and Chris laughed out of relief.

She checked her "about" information, and it listed her employment as The Gal's Bar and Grill. Another quick search gave her the address, and she started her car to head down, out of the Hollywood Hills.

Just after eleven thirty that night, Chris walked into The Gal's Bar and Grill, a small, trendy establishment just off Santa Monica Boulevard. The place was fairly full of people, mostly businesswomen, drinking at the mahogany bar and small tables, eating what looked like tapas.

All Chris had to go by were the photographs she'd seen on Natalie's Facebook page, but no one looked like her. She stepped up to the bar and got the bartender's attention.

"I'm looking for Natalie Crowden."

The tall blond woman raised her eyebrows and then said, "Friend or foe?"

That was a bit peculiar. "Neither."

"Cop?"

"No." She didn't need to know everything.

The bartender looked her over as if trying to decide whether she was going to cause trouble or not. "In the back," she finally said, "through that door." She jerked her head toward the far wall and then turned to a customer that waved a twenty-dollar bill at her.

The sound of the bar's music faded just slightly as Chris closed the back door behind her. A woman sat in a tiny office, going over some kind of paperwork. Without lifting her head, she said, "Out of wine already?"

"No." Chris stepped into the office.

It was definitely Natalie.

"May I help you?"

"I'm Chris Bergstrom. I was wondering—"

"Sarah's Chris?"

"Yes."

"You're the police officer?"

"I am."

Natalie studied her. "She likes you."

"That's really good to hear." Chris shifted her weight from one foot to the other. "Have you seen her lately?"

"No. I talked to her a few days ago, but she hasn't returned my calls since then."

"I can't seem to reach her either."

Again, Natalie scrutinized her. This was a mildly paranoid place, Chris thought.

"Close the door," Natalie said, "and sit down."

The only chair was so close, they could have shared a TV dinner without having to pass it back and forth.

"Sarah," Natalie said, "has had a rough time."

"Is she okay?"

"Her grandmother passed away Wednesday."

"Momo…"

"You met her? She was a kick in the pants."

"Oh, that's horrible," Chris said. "It seemed she was the only family member she was close to."

"She was. Momo kept her from going over the deep end many times."

"I went by the Pullmans' house and her mother didn't say a thing about the death. Not that she should have, necessarily. I'd only met her once."

"Once is enough."

"Yeah, I was there for Father's Day and it became a bit of a scene."

"Nothing surprising."

"Anyway, her mother said she hadn't seen Sarah either."

"Given what happened, that'd be the last place she'd go."

"What do you mean?"

Natalie's lips pinched together and she looked down.

Chris's worry rose. "What happened?"

"She never told you." It was a statement.

"Told me what?"

Natalie looked up, almost staring at her. Something was going on, and maybe it had to do with where Sarah was now.

"Please," Chris said.

"When Sarah was about eleven years old," Natalie said slowly, "she was kidnapped."

"What?!"

"It was some executive ransom thing. Her father was a fat cat, strutting his money around the city, and these guys followed her to school and took her."

"Oh, my God."

"Her father at first doubted that it was a real kidnapping. When her sweater was sent to them after a week or so, he finally coughed up the money."

"Was she hurt?"

"They kept her tied up and beat the crap out of her. Thank God they didn't rape her. But the entire time, she thought she was going to die. They caught the guys and she had to go to court for the trial. That was just as hard for her because she said she blocked out a lot of the kidnapping. But the worst thing was that her father still didn't seem that concerned. He treated it all like a business deal, and when it was done, he went back to his normal life. So after all that, she kind of disconnected. I don't think she's ever trusted much of anything since then."

Chris couldn't imagine how it would feel to have your parents do nothing to save you while you sat in fear for a week. She pictured Sarah, alone and scared for her life, and her entire body broke out in chills.

"We met about eight years after that," Natalie said. "She was a wild one, I tell you. She didn't care about anything. But I think she was kind of lost. I mean, she would try this and then try that. She always seemed to be searching for who she was."

Suddenly, something Sarah said came back to her. The last night they'd talked, she'd told Chris that she was a faceless person. She also said, the one thing she couldn't quite remember was the thing she couldn't forget. Chris ached to get to her. She had to be in a bad state, and though Chris's own idiotic words had made it worse, she still needed to find her.

Natalie picked up a pen and rolled it idly in her fingers. "Sarah has joked about having PTSD, but she does have it. That whole experience comes back to her often. I can tell, because when it happens, she goes off and does something irrational."

"Do you have *any* idea where she might be?"

Natalie shook her head. "When she called me, she wasn't in a good place. I tried to get her to come over, but she wouldn't. She's prone to disappearing when she's feeling fucked up, but all I could do was tell her I loved her and to call me soon."

"I just want to find her."

"She'll come back, Chris. She just needs time."

Chris wasn't so sure. "I'm just worried that her grandmother's death was pretty traumatic for her."

"You're right," Natalie said. "She's never lost a family member before, especially not someone as close to her as Momo."

Natalie took the pen and wrote on a scrap of paper, then handed it to her. "This is my cell number. Call me if you find her. And give me yours."

Chris told her and Natalie wrote it down.

When Chris got up, she said, "Thank you for trusting me enough to tell me."

Natalie looked at her again, and Chris then understood that all the assessment came from the need to protect her friend. Chris liked that a lot.

Natalie picked up some paper, ready to get back to work. "I can see that you care for her a lot. She needs that."

❖

Back in her car, Chris tried to collect her thoughts. It seemed noteworthy that Natalie hadn't been able to reach her either. Sure, Sarah was under a lot of stress, but wouldn't she at least talk to her best friend? The mother certainly hadn't helped with any information. She'd known about Momo's death when they'd spoke, but apparently she wasn't going to impart that bit of information. As significant as Sarah's grandmother's death was, maybe Mrs. Pullman just didn't approve of Chris. It was also possible that the Pullmans weren't naturally forthright people.

What the hell was going on? Chris then wondered if the better question was, what the hell had happened to Sarah between Momo's death and now?

She wasn't locked up in her room, refusing to answer the phone for anyone. Her car was gone, but she could be anywhere. The thought of Sarah driving when she was so distressed scared her. She knew from her job that people in shock never paid attention when they got behind the wheel. She'd seen too many…

She started her car. It was a ridiculous endeavor, but Chris pulled out into traffic and headed downtown.

❖

She walked up to the front desk and waited for the man behind it to look up.

"Hello, Officer," he said. "How may I help you?"

"May I speak to the deputy coroner, please?"

The man dialed a number and Chris stepped away. There was one main dull and drab hallway that was not only sterile from some overly potent disinfectant, but also barren from a lack of artwork or colorful patterned carpet. The doors she could see looked tired and heavy from age as well as the melancholy of Lord knows how many stories of people's lives and their ends.

Soon a tall gentleman in a lab coat over his Levi's came walking down the hall. He held out his hand to her. "Officer."

"Good evening. I've come by on a personal task. I was hoping you could tell me if any deceased females have been brought in during the past few days. Caucasian, mid-thirties, light-brown, shoulder-length hair, a purple tattoo of Chinese characters on the left shoulder?"

"No one that fits that description."

"Okay." Her relief was immense and she smiled nervously. "Thank you." She shook his hand. "I'm sorry for the interruption."

The deputy coroner waved his hand through the air. "No worries. I hope you find her."

"No offense, but I'm glad she's not with you."

He laughed and the echo sounded almost surreal. "None taken."

❖

She couldn't do anything else but go home. The haze of uncertainty and fear clouded her vision and muffled the traffic noises as she drove slowly down Sunset Boulevard. It surprised her when she ended up in her own driveway. She hadn't remembered any other cars on the road and wasn't even sure if she'd signaled at any turns.

You weren't there for her, she said silently. She had good reason not to call you, even after her grandmother died.

Chris plucked a vodka bottle from the kitchen counter and spun the cap until it flew off, clinking annoyingly on the floor. She took a swig, ignoring the splashes dripping down her throat.

"Good job, Bergstrom," she said. "You're just now realizing

that your black-and-white control issues might not be the best way to live your life, but now it's too late because the woman you truly want to change for is gone."

She took another swig and coughed. She looked at the bottle and glared.

"Fuck!" she yelled, and took another long swallow.

Her father had berated her on the phone about things he had no business talking about. How much more perfect did she need to be to gain his approval? She'd spent her whole life scooping out a hole in the sand, hoping to impress him, but no matter how hard or fast she dug, she never gained any headway because the soft sand at the sides would just fall inward, filling it again.

When was she going to break away from his reign over her? She'd always believed that one day, he'd give her a proud nod, pat her on the back, and say, "Good job, Chris." But if it wasn't going to come after graduating from college, or getting through the police academy, or even ten years on the force, it would never come at all.

The vodka warmed her hands. A slow rolling fog began its descent from her head, moving over her shoulders and toward her belly. She waited for the sensation she knew would engulf her, that pleasant feeling when her father's disappointment would fade and fade until it ceased to hurt her.

She thought about Sarah, smiling her wicked smile by the blackberries. And she could almost taste their first kiss. That incredible woman had suffered so much pain as a child, and the least of it were the cuts from her kidnapper's bindings.

The vodka bottle grew heavy, as if it had expanded in her hand. She looked at it again.

"And this is the way you deal with your shit," she said. "Nice."

She stood and forced her now-rubbery legs to the sink. Fishing out the trash can underneath, she dropped the bottle in, tied up the bag, and carried it outside.

The cool breeze greeted her and she looked up at the sky.

Maybe there wouldn't be any more fires in Los Angeles for the season. That would leave only one to take care of, and that one wouldn't be contained until she saw Sarah. As a matter of fact, if Sarah would consider being with her again, those flames would ignite again like nothing she'd ever felt before.

❖

Chris drove west, down Santa Monica Boulevard, hoping to God this would be her last call. If she got lucky, but most Friday nights she didn't, she wouldn't have a drawn-out situation where she'd have to put in overtime. But then again, what did she have to go home to?

The night before had been a frustrating study in tossing and turning. She wondered if counting each position she tried to relax in would have been as good as counting sheep. And who the fuck came up with the sheep thing, anyway? She was out of ideas for getting in touch with Sarah. The limbo she'd grown into was beating the crap out of her. She had no way to reach her, no action items, and no control.

If Sarah was trying to send a sign that she was done with her, maybe all this nothingness, this radio silence, was it. Perhaps she should just let it go.

But letting go would be agony. Chris rubbed her chest. If she really had to do that, the pain would probably cripple her.

Twenty minutes before her shift was supposed to be over, Chris arrived on scene and went inside a restaurant to talk to a complainant. She found him waiting just inside the front door.

"What's the problem?" Chris said.

"That man," the nicely dressed Asian man said as he jerked his thumb over his shoulder, "is crazy. He just walked in off the street and started rambling. He's making a scene and scaring my customers."

She looked around the restaurant, and, in fact, most of the diners were more interested in what was going on in the back of the room than they were in their food. The man wore an untucked plaid shirt, dirty tan trousers, and athletic shoes that someone else had probably thrown away.

"I'll be back to get more information from you," she said, and walked toward the man.

He was apparently talking to no one but gestured as if he were. "Do you know I have a monopoly over the coffee industry? That's the problem, the complaint, right? And no one else knows what to eat. I eat eggs. Do you eat eggs? Is that the big problem?"

She'd seen many people like this. The code was 5150, which allowed peace officers, among other qualified people, to confine a person currently having a mental disorder, making them a danger to themselves or others or, in this case, if they appeared gravely disabled. His speech pattern indicated to Chris that he was probably schizophrenic.

"Sir, I'm Officer Bergstrom and I'd like to talk to you. Would you like to go outside?"

"I do nothing and that's what I do. Nothing," the man said. His face jerked to one side as if he'd bitten his tongue. "They put little needles in my scalp and they have this special equipment they touch me with. When they pulled the needles, I had a thought. Jesus knows what it is."

Chris kept her voice calm and pointed her open hand toward the front door. "Let's go outside, okay?"

Wiping both arms at the same time, he said, "Outside. There are scales outside. Wet scales. All over. Do you understand what wet scales do? That's the problem."

"What's your name?"

He shuddered once and then reached up and twisted his hair. "Bill. I'm doing it. I'm lost, aren't I?"

"Bill, come on, let's go outside."

"I can't. This is a sanctuary. The sanctuary of Jesus."

"I have a protector out there. It's my protector dog, Abel."

He dangled his right hand at his hip and shook it back and forth. "Does Abel know Jesus?"

"Yes, he does."

Though his face remained emotionless and seemingly uncomprehending, Bill began walking slowly and Chris followed him out.

She took him over to her car and Abel barked. Bill jumped but began laughing. "He's protecting me!"

"He is," Chris said as she spoke quietly into her radio, calling for the dispatcher to send the psychological evaluation team.

"What's his name?"

"Abel." The man wasn't showing any signs of aggression so all she had to do was keep him there, and calm, until the PET team arrived.

"Dogs can hear the signals under Earth."

"What signals are those?"

"Magnetic messages that are transferred by protons in the dirt. They're the same protons that are in your brain. Dogs pick them up. Over my head, the needles stick in and try to extract protons. Dogs are immune."

"So, you like Abel?"

"Yes."

"What's your last name, Bill?"

"Hollywood has rotting lettuce under its streets. It decays and the smell goes into the ozone. Sidewalks leak. That's the problem."

"This sidewalk is safe, Bill."

"Maybe. Maybe." He began shaking his right hand again.

Abel wouldn't stop barking, but Bill didn't seem to mind.

"Where do you live, Bill?"

He kept looking into her car but moved his arm back, pointing to either the building or the sidewalk. "Here."

If he wasn't talking about rotting lettuce again, he was probably letting her know he was homeless.

A nondescript ambulance showed up and pulled over in front of Chris's car. She briefed them, and as they began to work with him, she went back into the restaurant and got the owner's name and details of the call. She stuffed her pad of paper into her front pocket and came back out as they were putting Bill on the gurney in the back of the ambulance.

She leaned into the back. "You take care, Bill."

"Your dog knows. He has the same protons as a werewolf. You watch him tonight."

"I will," Chris said, and started to turn away.

"It's a full moon tonight. That's the problem, it's the complaint, isn't it?"

Chris stopped suddenly, her feet frozen to the ground. She turned back around to look at Bill. His face twitched as he started talking to the mental-health-care technician. The driver closed the ambulance door.

Abruptly, Chris rushed back to her car, put it in gear, and flicked on the siren and light bar. She made a tight U-turn in the middle of the boulevard and sped off.

She raced home to drop off her car and kennel Abel. Then she rushed to change her clothes and grab a few things, and jumped into her other car.

❖

There had to be a closer street, she thought, as she reached the end of Beachwood Boulevard, high up in the hills. She sat at the end of the residential street where it turned into a dirt road leading to a stable where tourists could rent horses. She turned around and zigzagged her way around the curvy neighborhood roads until she came upon Mulholland Way.

This was a better place. She drove a ways past the last house, up two short S-curves, to a part of the road that was too steep on both sides for any home construction and, effectively, devoid of traffic. She patted her pocket to confirm she had her cell phone and flashlight and got out of the car.

She walked back down the dark road to the last house and looked up. A couple of streetlamps lighted the bottom of the hill, but then the vegetation disappeared into blackness. A small interruption in the bushes looked like a trail, and she began her ascent.

In almost complete blackness, her climb was slow going. The full moon was bright but offered little light for topography that was not only completely unfamiliar but far from hospitable. It was a complete crapshoot, but she had to go. The trail was incredibly steep, and she held her hands out because she knew she might fall. She slipped a few times in the loose dirt and felt prickly thorns rake her hands.

After ten minutes or so, the bushes seemed to fall away and a crunching sound came from under her feet. She turned her flashlight on, covering the light with her hand, to avoid drawing attention to herself. A fire had been through at some point and burned away a lot of the brush.

She continued up, losing ground a couple of times as rocks flipped out from under her feet, clacking and banging as they rolled down the hill. Her hands stung from the thorns, and now, the brush that had evaded the fire sliced her arms. She stopped and flicked the flashlight on again. The trail was gone. She didn't risk shining the light above her to see where she needed to go, so she kept climbing, damning herself for not wearing long sleeves.

Sweat trickled down her face and dampened her shirt. Her thighs and calves protested the onslaught of mild aching that would be a lot worse the next day, but she was already more than half the way up.

For the next fifteen minutes, a succession of five steps up only to slide four back down frustrated her. She couldn't see much and wasn't even sure, other than up, if she was going in the right direction.

A thumping sound, low and foreboding, broke through the cadence of her heavy breathing. She stopped, turning left and right, in order to locate the source.

It was high in the air, which meant one thing. She hunkered down and finally spotted the helicopter making a sweep of the hills.

"Shit," she said, having nowhere to hide if the chopper decided to use its spotlight to search for people just like her. Had somebody seen her start her climb? Had they called the police? As the helicopter got closer, a jolt of fear raced through her. She was breaking the law, and if she got caught, she could lose her job.

On her knees, still trying to catch her breath, she stared at the ground, listening to the thwacking of the rotor blades. After a minute or two, she looked up. They appeared to be on a general search because, if they'd had a specific target, they'd be flying a lot lower.

Finally, the helicopter tilted to its left and made a plunging arc, heading back down toward Hollywood. Still, she waited a few minutes, unwilling to press her luck too soon.

From somewhere else a ways away, the brush made a thrashing sound. There were many deer in the area, and she hoped that's what it was. Otherwise, she might be coming face-to-face with a bobcat.

She started to move again but the terrain had gotten much steeper. She was bent over, using her hands to scramble up and dropping to her knees when gravity was winning.

The screech of a hawk startled her, and she got her flashlight back out of her pocket, just in case. She wasn't worried that the hawk would come swooping down on her head, but she wanted to be ready in case she accidentally met any rodents or small animals that the hawk was looking for.

Finally, she was able to stand upright and found a small animal-made trail. She followed it, gaining more altitude, and after the next ten minutes, she stopped. Towering above her was the one thing she'd seen almost every day of her life but had never gotten close to or touched.

Nine immense structures, forty-five feet tall, spelled out the word HOLLYWOOD in white, corrugated steel.

She hiked up the last hundred feet, reaching the letter D. Stepping behind the sign, she stopped to let her lungs calm down again.

The view was spectacular. Hollywood, and Los Angeles beyond that, spread out in a beautiful pattern of twinkling lights and lines of white and red cars on the streets and boulevards.

But she wasn't on this joyride to sightsee. She made her way past the letters as quietly as she could, careful to avoid the small, silhouetted rectangles that perched on the top of some of the letters. Those had to be security cameras.

Just under the first L, she found her. Sarah sat huddled against the steel posts holding up the letter. Her head was down on her knees, her arms wrapped around her legs. She didn't turn toward her as Chris stepped up.

She knelt and realized she was asleep. "Sarah."

Slowly, Sarah raised her head and looked at her.

"Chris," she said slowly, "What are you doing here?"

Looking up to the sky, she said, "It's a full moon."

"Come here." Sarah took Chris's hand.

When she sat down next to her, Chris said, "That was a hell of a climb."

"You came up from the front?"

"Yeah. Why?"

Sarah pointed behind her at a faint outline of a fence about fifty feet away. "All you have to do is take the trail that starts at Beachwood Drive and come around the back side of Mt. Lee. Then you can climb over the fence."

"Shit." Chris held her hands up. "I could have saved myself the loss of blood."

Sarah took her hands in her own. "Are you okay?"

"Yeah, yeah. I just needed to see you. You weren't answering your phone and I got worried."

"I think it's sitting at my house. I haven't had it for days."

Chris held on tight. "I am so sorry about Momo."

Even in the dark, Chris could see Sarah's face. It was drawn and her eyes were puffy from crying.

"I feel so lost without her. She was my sanity." Tears came and glimmered at the corners of her eyes. "They said she went in her sleep. I'm grateful for that."

"I'm glad you're okay. When I couldn't reach you, I didn't know what to do."

"I kind of went blank. I drove over to my parents' house after they called. They acted like the maid had just quit. They were pissed at the inconvenience of dealing with her." Sarah laughed, but the sound was tinged with sarcasm. "It didn't take them three seconds to start talking about how to redecorate her room."

"Jesus."

"I pretty much blew a gasket and told them all to go to hell and that I would make all the arrangements for her service and burial. I've been staying there pretty much since she died because I didn't want them to have anything to do with it."

"I'm so sorry, Sarah."

She lowered her head. "I know." Her voice had become so small.

"And I'm sorry about the last night I saw you."

She looked up at her. "I know that, too."

"I was stupid. And I've known for a long time that drinking when I get anxious or insecure is the worst thing I can do." She took a deep breath. She wouldn't be hiding behind a bottle any more. "I said really horrible things to you."

"It hurt."

"Sarah, please believe me when I say it's been the worst regret of my life."

"You're not that far off the truth, though."

"What do you mean?"

"I'm aware of my own self-fulfilling prophecy. I haven't been such a good person, and I know it's because I grew up under my parents' roof. They did everything but write on a Post-it Note that I was no good."

"That's bullshit."

"They made it clear more times than I can count that I wasn't the apple of their eye. Maybe if I'd turned into an apple martini…"

"And when I got drunk, it hit home, didn't it?" Making that connection slammed into Chris's chest, almost doubling her over in pain.

"The truth? Yes. But it wasn't a surprise. It's true that I don't have a career. And it's true that my parents support me. So when you said those things, they didn't surprise me. It made sense, actually."

"What made sense?"

"That you would see me that way. It's because I have no identity. I don't know who I am."

"What I said, I said because I was afraid. I lashed out at you because you were different. I never meant for you to think you were a nobody or that you weren't important. You *are*. And I see that, Sarah. You are someone special, and I see you for the incredible woman you are."

"That night, when I left your house," Sarah said, "I decided I had to stop seeing you. You were right about me, and I wasn't going to live up to your standards."

"My standards are fucked up. I don't want to see the world the way I have been." Chris's heart surged and an overwhelming burst of desire overcame her. "There's no excuse for what I said to you, but I can tell you that I did it because I was afraid. And then I couldn't find you and all these questions came. What do you do when you think you've found the perfect woman for you? What do you do when all you can think about is her—how she is, what she's doing right now, and whether she's smiling that intoxicating smile? What do you do when you can't seem to breathe without her?"

She turned to look out over the nighttime panorama that stretched below them. Her throat constricted and she just let the tears come. She was ashamed of her behavior and the hurt she'd caused Sarah. And she realized that not only did she have to cut the strict bindings she'd tightened around her life, but she had to burn them to ashes.

Chris wiped the tears from her eyes and looked back at Sarah. "I've never met anyone as out there, as brave and fearless enough to live out loud and break the rules as you."

"How could you want someone who's so unlike you? I don't have anything to offer."

"You can't believe that."

"You don't know everything about me."

"Sarah," Chris said, unsure how to tell her. There'd be time to say everything about that night, but for now, she kept it brief. "I found Natalie. I was desperate to see you. She told me about the kidnapping."

Sarah nodded knowingly. She raised her head, looking skyward, and then sniffed as if she'd sadly abandoned the onset of a laugh. "When I was a little girl, I wanted the fairy tale. I wasn't sure what that was, but it had to be the exact opposite of what I saw between my parents. And then my world changed.

"Strangers took me when I was playing out in front of my house. They covered my head and drove for a long time. I remember after they finally got me out of the car, they dragged me inside some house. All I remember was the smell of trash and cigarettes. They tied me up in a room and told me they'd kill me if I screamed.

"The first night I was there, I got out of the ropes and they caught me climbing out a window. There was one big guy who beat me up. He kept yelling and smacking my face. My nose hurt so badly and was all bloody. When he finally stopped, he shoved a gun just under my cheek and told me he'd blow my head off if I tried anything again.

"By then I was so scared, I wouldn't even ask to use the bathroom. I sat there wondering when my parents would come get me and take me home. After the big guy beat me up the first night, a shorter guy started coming in to bring me food and stuff, but the big guy would come in a few times a day and point the gun at me, just to make sure I didn't try to escape again. The shorter guy seemed to be pissed that the big guy hit me, but I knew the big guy was in charge.

"As time went on, I thought they'd get sick of waiting. Every time the door would open, I'd start to shake because I knew they'd point the gun at me one last time and kill me. But do you know what the worst part about the whole thing was? Did Natalie tell you my father didn't believe I was actually kidnapped and waited two weeks to have me rescued?"

Chris slowly nodded.

"Well, that wasn't the worst part. The shorter guy, the one that brought me food, came to check on me every few hours. He'd come in the room and ask if I was okay. If I needed water, he'd bring it. He checked my nose when it bled and gave me paper towels. Every day, he'd say, 'Are you okay?'" She began to cry again. "My parents never did that." A small snort came from Sarah as she shook her head. "They never tucked me in. Never asked me if I was okay. So when I finally got home, I didn't want to be there. I sometimes wished I was still a hostage instead of being at home because at least that one kidnapper actually gave a shit."

"Oh, Sarah, I didn't know."

"No one knows. I never even told Natalie that part." She shuddered as she inhaled. "I was invisible to them. I lost who I was. I didn't care about anything after that. I did whatever I wanted and said whatever I wanted. They expected me to go to college and that's why I didn't go. They wanted a debutante and I turned into a hellion. Along the way, I became so good at rebelling just to rebel that I never figured out what *I* wanted to do and who I really was.

"And then I met you," Sarah said as she looked out over the city. "In past relationships, I found myself settling because I was comfortable. I wanted more than that. I wanted that one person who understands and sees my soul. The one who gives me those butterflies with just a glance, the one who gives me goose bumps with a touch. And when she holds me, any separation between us just blends into an unbreakable closeness, like we're one. I wanted you with the deepest parts of my being. I found all of that with you. But I was afraid you wouldn't want me because of who I am." Sarah turned to Chris. "Do you remember when I told you that I've experienced the worst and that nothing scares me anymore? I was wrong. Only one thing frightens me. And that's losing you."

"Sarah, I see who you are, and you're every bit as wonderful and beautiful as I could ever wish for," Chris said. "When we first met, I was scared because my own fucked-up rules didn't have room for someone as unique as you. I was afraid that being with you would affect me in a way I couldn't control. And the fact is, it did. But that's the kind of control I want to lose. I'm falling in love with you and I don't want to fight it."

"Do you really feel that way?"

"I do. I know you want to finally believe in someone, and I want to be the one. So, if you'll take a chance with me, I'll give you the fairy tale."

Sarah looked at her the way she had when they'd last made love. They kissed for the first time in what felt like years. Sarah's soft lips touched hers, and Chris swore she felt the angels blessing her with divine redemption.

Sarah pulled away and tenderly wiped Chris's lip with her thumb. "You remembered what I said about coming up here."

"I think I've remembered everything you've said." She

reached up with one hand and held her face. It was the most beautiful sight she could ever take in.

Sarah reached up to her shirtsleeve, pulling it up to reveal her tattoo. "Do you remember what this says?"

"Even in hell," Chris said, her heart feeling full, "angels can find you."

"You did."

She kissed her, tasting the possibility of forever. "I don't know if we're going to get down the hill without being arrested for trespassing, but I'd like to take you home and make love to you."

"I've coerced you into coming over to the dark side."

"Sometimes love is more important than following the rules."

"I'll remind you that you said that when I have another urge to sing karaoke on a rooftop."

"Don't be surprised if I hand you the microphone."

"I love you, Chris Bergstrom."

"And I love you, Sarah Pullman."

Chris stood and helped Sarah up. They took one last look out over the Los Angeles skyline. The fires had all been quashed, and the hills were starting their journey back to renewal and restoration. All things were possible in the City of Angels.

About the Author

Lisa Girolami has been in the entertainment industry since 1979. She holds a BA in fine art and an MS in psychology and is a licensed MFT specializing in LGBT clients. Previous jobs included ten years as a production executive in the motion picture industry and another two decades producing and designing theme parks for Disney and Universal Studios. She is now a director and senior producer with Walt Disney Imagineering.

Writing has been a passion for her since she wrote and illustrated her first comic books at the restless age of six. Her imagination usually gets the best of her, and plotting her next novel during boring corporate meetings keeps her from going stir-crazy. She currently lives in Long Beach, California.

Books Available From Bold Strokes Books

The Heat of Angels by Lisa Girolami. Fires burn in more than one place in Los Angeles. (978-1-62639-042-3)

Season of the Wolf by Robin Summers. Two women running from their pasts are thrust together by an unimaginable evil. Can they overcome the horrors that haunt them in time to save each other? (978-1-62639-043-0)

Desperate Measures by P. J. Trebelhorn. Homicide detective Kay Griffith and contractor Brenda Jansen meet amidst turmoil neither of them is aware of until murder suspect Tommy Rayne makes his move to exact revenge on Kay. (978-1-62639-044-7)

The Magic Hunt by L.L. Raand. With her Pack being hunted by human extremists and beset by enemies masquerading as friends, can Sylvan protect them and her mate, or will she succumb to the feral rage that threatens to turn her rogue, destroying them all? A Midnight Hunters novel. (978-1-62639-045-4)

Wingspan by Karis Walsh. Wildlife biologist Bailey Chase is content to live at the wild bird sanctuary she has created on Washington's Olympic Peninsula until she is lured beyond the safety of isolation by architect Kendall Pearson. (978-1-60282-983-1)

Night Bound by Winter Pennington. Kass struggles to keep her head, her heart, and her relationships in order. She's still having a difficult time accepting being an Alpha female—but her wolf is certain of what she wants and she's intent on securing her power. (978-1-60282-984-8)

The Blush Factor by Gun Brooke. Ice-cold business tycoon Eleanor Ashcroft only cares about the three Ps—Power, Profit, and Prosperity—until young Addison Garr makes her doubt both that and the state of her frostbitten heart. (978-1-60282-985-5)

Slash and Burn by Valerie Bronwen. The murder of a roundly despised author at an LGBT writers' conference in New Orleans turns Winter Lovelace's relaxing weekend hobnobbing with her peers into a nightmare of suspense—especially when her ex turns up. (978-1-60282-986-2)

The Quickening: A Sisters of Spirits novel by Yvonne Heidt. Ghosts, visions, and demons are all in a day's work for Tiffany. But when Kat asks for help on a serial killer case, life takes on another dimension altogether. (978-1-60282-975-6)

Windigo Thrall by Cate Culpepper. Six women trapped in a mountain cabin by a blizzard, stalked by an ancient cannibal demon bent on stealing their sanity—and their lives. (978-1-60282-950-3)

Smoke and Fire by Julie Cannon. Oil and water, passion and desire, a combustible combination. Can two women fight the fire that draws them together and threatens to keep them apart? (978-1-60282-977-0)

Love and Devotion by Jove Belle. KC Hall trips her way through life, stumbling into an affair with a married bombshell twice her age. Thankfully, her best friend, Emma Reynolds, is there to show her the true meaning of Love and Devotion. (978-1-60282-965-7)

The Shoal of Time by J.M. Redmann. It sounded too easy. Micky Knight is reluctant to take the case because the easy ones often turn into the hard ones, and the hard ones turn into the dangerous ones. In this one, easy turns hard without warning. (978-1-60282-967-1)

In Between by Jane Hoppen. At the age of fourteen, Sophie Schmidt discovers that she was born an intersexual baby and sets off on a journey to find her place in a world that denies her true existence. (978-1-60282-968-8)

Under Her Spell by Maggie Morton. The magic of love brought Terra and Athene together, but now a magical quest stands between them—a quest for Athene's hand in marriage. Will their passion keep them together, or will stronger magic tear them apart? (978-1-60282-973-2)

Rush by Carsen Taite. Murder, secrets, and romance combine to create the ultimate rush. (978-1-60282-966-4)

Scars by Amy Dunne. While fleeing from her abuser, Nicola Jackson bumps into Jenny O'Connor, and their unlikely friendship quickly develops into a blossoming romance—but when it comes down to a matter of life or death, are they both willing to face their fears? (978-1-60282-970-1)

Homestead by Radclyffe. R. Clayton Sutter figures getting NorthAm Fuel's newest refinery operational on a rolling tract of land in upstate New York should take a month or two, but then, she hadn't counted on local resistance in the form of vandalism, petitions, and one furious farmer named Tess Rogers. (978-1-60282-956-5)

Battle of Forces: Sera Toujours by Ali Vali. Kendal and Piper return to New Orleans to start the rest of eternity together, but the return of an old enemy makes their peaceful reunion short-lived, especially when they join forces with the new queen of the vampires. (978-1-60282-957-2)

How Sweet It Is by Melissa Brayden. Some things are better than chocolate. Molly O'Brien enjoys her quiet life running the bakeshop in a small town. When the beautiful Jordan Tuscana returns home, Molly can't deny the attraction—or the stirrings of something more. (978-1-60282-958-9)

The Missing Juliet: A Fisher Key Adventure by Sam Cameron. A teenage detective and her friends search for a kidnapped Hollywood star in the Florida Keys. (978-1-60282-959-6)

Amor and More: Love Everafter, edited by Radclyffe and Stacia Seaman. Rediscover favorite couples as Bold Strokes Books authors reveal glimpses of life and love beyond the honeymoon in short stories featuring main characters from favorite BSB novels. (978-1-60282-963-3)

First Love by CJ Harte. Finding true love is hard enough, but for Jordan Thompson, daughter of a conservative president, it's challenging, especially when that love is a female rodeo cowgirl. (978-1-60282-949-7)

Pale Wings Protecting by Lesley Davis. Posing as a couple to investigate the abduction of infants, Special Agent Blythe Kent and Detective Daryl Chandler find themselves drawn into a battle over the innocents, with demons on one side and the unlikeliest of protectors on the other. (978-1-60282-964-0)